I0623822

Tales from the Canyons of the Damned

DANIEL ARTHUR SMITH

Tales from the Canyons of the Damned No. 19

First Edition

Special thanks to Jessica West

ISBN-13: 978-1946777430 ISBN-10: 1946777439

Cover By Daniel Arthur Smith

Horror Fiction from Holt Smith ltd
Agroland
Tower

~*~

For Susan, Tristan, & Oliver, as all things are.

~*~

Carving in the Pumpkin Patch
Christopher J. Valin

~*~

I TOLD MYSELF, "This time it will be different." And it was.

Because that was when the murders began.

I was sitting in the pumpkin patch like I did every Halloween. No costume, no candy, no eggs to throw at houses. But I had a plan to make sure I wasn't alone this Halloween.

It wasn't quite a full moon, but it was close enough and really bright, which added to the holiday atmosphere. I built a little fire in a clearing, small enough that it couldn't be seen from the road or other parts of the farm. There were still some pumpkins out there even though most of them had been sold over the past couple of weeks, and I was really getting into the spirit as I popped open a can.

I had given the homeless guy forty bucks to get me a case of light beer at the liquor store where he hung out. Told him he could keep the rest.

Then I bought a quarter ounce of weed and some 'shrooms from the skeevy kid we used to make fun of for being dirty and smelly back in elementary school. Damn, we were cruel. I felt sorry for him, but never enough to step up and defend him. No wonder he became a dropout dealer by the age of sixteen. I really lucked out having a sister who beat the shit out of anyone who made fun of me, since I had some serious issues of my own. Way worse than just not showering often enough, like that poor bastard.

Honestly, I can't even remember his real name.

We all had nicknames by the time we were in middle school. Mine was Thumbelina. It was supposed to be clever because it referenced one of my fixations *and* my actual name, which is no prize itself. I don't know what the hell my parents were thinking, but they didn't do me any favors. No wonder I was so messed up. Luckily, everyone got tired of saying such a long name all the time, and it was shortened to just Lee.

The only ones who were allowed to say anything to me about my weird habits were those in our core group of friends. And my sister herself, of course. Other than protecting me, she'd always been a pretty mean bitch—to me and almost everyone else. Except Piano Man. But he ignored her most of the time, unless he was drunk. Then they'd head off into the back seat of his car for a while. Next day, he was back to acting like he didn't even know her.

Like with most bullies, nobody liked my sister, but she was always around because everyone was too afraid to tell her to leave. She treated my best friend the worst, since he was an easy target. Plus, he would just take it, over and over again, and never respond or snitch on her.

I always wondered if maybe he secretly had a thing for her. Or just enjoyed being punished. Like, maybe he was some kind of masochist. I know if someone treated *me* that way for long enough, I'd probably snap at some point.

Since we were too old to trick-or-treat now, it wasn't all that difficult to get the others to come hang out with me in the pumpkin patch. I hadn't mentioned my annual vigil in years, so I'm sure they'd all forgotten about it, even though they used to tease me mercilessly. It seemed normal to them to find a place where we could hide out and party. We did it all the time.

This year, everyone would have a good time, and I would still get to sit and wait and quiet that little voice. Every Halloween, I'd make an excuse not to go out with the rest of them. Then I'd sit out here by myself and hope it was finally going to happen. It never did, but it was totally a compulsion at that point. I'd think, *Forget about it. Just go out with you friends for once.* And the voice inside my head would say, *Sure. Don't go. But this'll be the year. And you'll miss it after all that time you wasted.*

The little voice always wins out.

So, I hooked some battery-powered speakers up to my phone and blasted some metal, then waited for my friends to show. Not that any of them would ever be on time. Except maybe Pat and her girlfriend. They'd usually be punctual if there was pot involved. She'd actually kick my ass if I ran out before she got any.

I just hoped Sal wouldn't show up. Not only was she my best friend's kid sister, but she'd had a crush on me practically our whole lives. I finally thought maybe I was rid of her when I heard she was going out with someone her own age. Then I screwed up a couple of weeks ago when I was wasted and made out with her at her house when their parents were out of town.

Now I'd probably never be rid of her.

I grabbed my carving knife and started working on the jack-o-lantern while I waited. I had found the biggest, roundest pumpkin I could and pulled out all the guts. Instead of carving a lid in the top, I carved a big opening in the bottom. This wasn't going to be sitting on anyone's doorstep with a candle lighting it up. I was planning on wearing it on my head and jumping out at my friends once they were good and stoned. Scare the crap out of them. Hopefully literally. Having them shit their pants in fear would be sweet vengeance for making fun of me all those years.

But even if it just gave them a good scare for a few seconds, it would be worth it.

I had a few pizzas waiting for them, and little did they know that the mushrooms on them were the fun kind. It wasn't like they were going to hurt anyone or anything. All natural, right?

The first one to show up was actually Piano Man. He was a chill dude, other than his taste in music. "How can you listen to this crap?"

"It's not crap. Just because it's not classical doesn't mean it isn't any good."

"Believe me, it does."

"You want some beer or not? I'm not putting any stupid Beethoven on. Nobody else will stick around if I do." I handed him a beer.

"Sure. I'll try to tune out this garbage." He grabbed the beer and popped it open, taking a giant swig right off the bat. "Is your, uh, sister coming?"

"I hope not. But if she does, don't even think about it, man. It's really jacked up how you only pay attention to her when you're drinking. Then she gets pissed and takes it out on everyone else. Especially me."

He shrugged and took another gulp.

Pat and her girl showed up soon after, just as I expected. She didn't want any beer and brought her own wine coolers. But she asked about my weed immediately, and I hooked her up. It always freaked me out a little how her girlfriend called her "Sir," but I guess everyone has their own thing. Was she her lover or her boss? Anyway, I had to make sure they didn't go through it all before the rest arrived.

Chuck's sister, Sal, was next, but she wasn't alone. She had gotten a ride from Frank, and he had his arm around her as they walked over to the little clearing where we were hanging out. Instead of feeling relieved, I actually felt a little jealous for some reason. I mean, yeah, she was starting to get cuter, sure. And that blonde hair...

What the hell was wrong with me?

I handed Frank a beer, and Sal held out her hand.

"I don't know. Is Chuck going to be mad at me if I let you drink?"

Frank grabbed a beer away from me and handed it to her. "Oh, she's drinking, man. Ain't your decision." They walked away before I could even respond. She turned back and gave me a look. A weird look and a smile. I didn't know what to make of it.

I pulled out the pizza and opened up the boxes. They all dug in, mushrooms and all. This was definitely going to be fun.

Everyone was starting to really mellow out and relax. Other than the music, everything was quiet as they stared into the fire. The 'shrooms were working their magic. I really wanted to wait for Chuck before I did my scare prank, but I could tell some people were going to be leaving soon, and he hadn't responded to any of my texts or calls. I got tired of walking back to the main road just to get some service to check and see if he'd gotten back to me.

My sister wasn't there either, but that was probably just as well, since she'd kick the crap out of me for sure after I scared her. And it grossed me out whenever she got together with Piano Man, too.

So, I snuck out into the patch, where I had my pumpkin head ready. I also had some old clothes I'd ripped up to give the full effect. When I pulled it over my head, it was hard to breathe, and even harder to see. And, even though I'd cleaned it out well, there was still goop inside. Oh well, it would all be worth it when I saw their faces.

But as I was walking back around to figure out the best place to approach the clearing I tripped over something. It was hard to tell what it was with the pumpkin over my head, but when I looked down, there it was.

My sister's body. Lying in a puddle of blood with her throat slit. Her dark hair was matted with red, and her eyes were wide open, a look of terror permanently fixed on her face.

Obviously, I figured out that it was a Halloween prank she was pulling on me. I hit her arm and told her to get up. But then I noticed how pale she was, and when I tried to feel for a pulse there was nothing. And the giant gash in her throat was real.

I screamed and tried to get up, sliding around in the crimson pool surrounding my sister's body, which had turned the soil to mud. I ran back into the clearing, still screaming, and everyone else started screaming at first, too. But after a second, they realized it was just me in a pumpkin head and started laughing.

Frank threw his half-full can of beer at me. "You freakin' loser! You look ridiculous A.F."

"No! You don't get it. I just found Lu's body. Someone killed her!"

They continued to laugh at how stupid I looked, and there was no way I was going to convince them after what just happened. They'd have to see it for themselves.

Piano Man, Pat, and what's-her-name agreed to follow me over to see the body, even though they were skeptical. But when we got there, she was gone, and the only sign that she'd been there was the puddle of blood.

Piano Man punched me in the shoulder. "You're an asshole man. I know what this is all about. It's that Giant Pumpkin thing you used to be obsessed with."

"It's not the *Giant* Pumpkin, it's the Gre—"

Pat interrupted. "Whatever! This is still bullshit. Isn't it, Mar—" She turned around and her girlfriend was gone. "Where'd she go? She was right behind me."

I grabbed both of them by the arm. "We need to stick together."

Pat pulled away and took off. "I'm gonna find her."

Piano Man looked at me like I was a complete psycho. "This is messed up. You're freaking everyone out. I'm outta here." He walked off in the other direction.

I heard a *thunk*, then a *thump*. "Piano Man?"

Just a few yards into the patch, he was lying face down, not moving. "Hey, I was serious about Lu. Stop messing with me. We need to get help."

Piano Man still didn't move. I shook him. Then rolled him over.

His throat was slit also. I jumped back, looking around. Whoever did this had to be right there with me. It had *just* happened.

I ran back to the clearing, but it sounded like nobody was left there. Then I saw that I was wrong. Frank was lying dead on top of Sal, like he'd been trying to protect her.

Only he didn't have a head.

Sal was still alive, but she was in a state of shock, unable to speak and completely drenched in blood. I dragged her out from under Frank and tried to get her to stand. She couldn't take her eyes off of Frank's headless corpse and refused to get up.

"There's no cell phone service out here. I'm going to go get help." Since I couldn't drag her, I started running to my car, but right away Sal started screaming back at the clearing. I couldn't just leave her to face whoever was killing my friends, so I sprinted back as fast as I could.

When I got back to the clearing again, Pat was coming out of the darkness, carrying her girlfriend's lifeless body. She shuffled forward a few steps, then fell down face first in the dirt. My carving knife was sticking out of her back.

Sal continued to scream and I put my arm around her, trying to calm her down. Then a dark figure came from the other direction, running toward us with its giant, round head.

I grabbed my knife out of Pat's back and barreled toward the figure, plunging my knife into its stomach with all my might before it could kill me. I stepped back as the figure stumbled toward the fire, revealing my best friend Chuck, a look of confusion scrawled across his face. He fell straight into the fire, causing it to flare up as his yellow and black sweater burst into flames.

I went back to Sal, but she just kept screaming and backing away from me.

I tried to hold onto her. To comfort her. But she was inconsolable. How could she not be? I wondered what had really happened. Had Chuck snapped and killed everyone? Or had I just made a terrible mistake?

The answer came seconds later, as another figure entered the clearing on the other side of the now-raging fire. At first, I couldn't tell who—or even what—it was. It was so covered in dirt and blood that it didn't even look human. But when he got closer, I could see his eyes, and realized I should have known all along.

As he raised his own knife and slashed it across my throat and I started to bleed out, my last thought was, "I still can't remember his real name…"

~*~

James and the
Great Pumpkin
(Carving Contest)
Kevin Lauderdale

~*~

IT IS A FACT universally acknowledged that a chap can never have too much of the ready stuff. I mean, of course, cash. Brass in pocket. The folding paper. Even a cove like myself, who might be said to be "in funds" or "a young man of independent means" (or, as my Aunt Agnes prefers, "a reprobate layabout who's never done a lick of work in his life") could always use a little more. Do you know what petrol costs these days? And cognac? It's obscene.

In the United States, where I am about to lay my scene, filthy lucre is delightfully colourful. All the bills have a lovely green tint, rather like the patina on the Statue of Liberty. Hence, a Broadway *boulevardier* (Is that the word I want? It doesn't mean "streetwalker," does it?

James assures me it does not. More of James anon.) who keeps up with slang has pockets full of "kale," "lettuce," or "cabbage." And yet is still in need of more. James and I were in New York—

I might as well settle the matter of James right now. My valet, don't you know. My personal gentleman's gentleman. General factotum: Chef for Yours Truly, Drink Mixer, Packer of Suitcases, Maker of Railroad Reservations, and My Shoe Shiner. And, as anyone who has read my earlier memoirs will recall, Solver of Problems.

If I had a dollar for every time James has extracted Reggie Brubaker (yours truly) and/or some pal of mine (too numerous to mention) from a jam, I'd be on such intimate relations with President Washington that I would use his first name. Despite his being a traitorous colonial.

James and I were in New York at the request of an old school chum of mine, Viscount Woodson, "Woody" to his fellow Old Etonians. We were exact contemporaries at Eton and Oxford, and, despite his tender years, Woody was the chief backer of a Broadway musical that he insisted was going to earn a mint-full…of mint. (I've just coined that slang term. Still green, but better-smelling than cabbage.) I'd travelled 3,500 miles from London to determine if this was something I'd want to invest in. Plus, I needed a couple of shirts.

Devoted patron that I am of Savile Row tailors for suits, I must admit that only Brooks Brothers has just the right shade of pink and just the right roll to their button-down collars.

We met outside the New Empire Theatre on Broadway and 46th at noon on a late October day.

"Hullo, Reggie," said Woody.

"Hullo, Woody," I replied. "Looks promising so far."

Everywhere people were running about lifting barges and toting bales. Men in shirtsleeves and flat caps who called everyone they met "Buddy" shifted scenery and rolled racks of flashy costumes. A dozen lovely young women in shorts and tops tied at the waist marched by as if on parade, their legs on display, their postures perfect. Ah, the sublimity of the legitimate theatre!

"So, what's this extravaganza called?" I asked. "What's it about?"

Woody scratched his head. "Well, that's the thing of it, old man." He frowned. "As near as I can figure, it's about a girl named Catherine who lives in Hawaii and makes a good living dancing."

"Haven't you read the thing?" I asked. Clearly this was the first step in any investment strategy. You don't plonk down at the race course without first giving the horses the once-over.

"Not as such. I'm just the backer. We've got a stage manager who covers all the details. But I'm sure it'll be a hit. My fiancée Kitty is in the chorus."

"Have you got the script?"

"Sure thing, old man." He dug into his camel hair coat and pulled out a rolled-up sheaf of pages. The three brass fasteners along one side proclaimed this to be a script. The cover was purple.

I tried to pronounce the title. *"The Call of...Cat's...Hulu?"*

"Yes," said Woody. "The author is some chap over in Rhode Island. Cat, that's the girl, I imagine. The Call, she's luring in lots of business. Hulu, Hawaiian dance."

"Isn't that 'hula'?"

Woody scratched his head. "Funny thing. Everyone I meet pronounces the title differently."

"Hard to sell tickets if your audience doesn't know how to ask for them," I said.

"Oh, there's been shows with worse names than this before. Remember *Hitchy-Koo* or *Biff! Bing! Bang!* with exclamation marks? They ran for a long time."

He had a point. Both New York's Broadway and London's West End were strewn with the corpses of shows that had been hits despite off-putting or confusing titles. *Animal Crackers,* for instance, had had nothing to do with biscuits. And the less said about *Little Miss Bluebeard*—which did not involve pirates, but was in fact a bedroom farce—the better.

"Look, Reggie," said Woody, "here's the goods…Oh, nice shirt by the way."

"Thanks," I replied. "Brooks. Goes well with my periwinkle tie, don't you think?"

"Like a treat. Anyway, we're all set for the opening. The rent, costumes, lights, etc. are all covered. We just need a little more money for incidentals."

"What sort of incidentals?" I asked.

"The cast and crew. None of them have been paid."

I glanced through the open door and into the New Empire. To say there was a cast of thousands milling about inside, some dancing on stage, some working the ropes and sandbags, would be an exaggeration. But not by much.

"Exactly how much do you need?" I asked. I couldn't tell if the show was actually set on a tropical island, but, if so, I imagined palm trees did not come cheap. Not to mention the fellows who moved the lights and painted the backdrops. I could see a couple of said fellows now. They were beefy. They looked like they enjoyed eating regularly and like all that food went directly to the development and maintenance of their muscles. They did not look the type to be satisfied with IOUs.

"Only two or three thousand," said Woody.

"Two or three thousand dollars!" I exclaimed. You could buy a Cadillac for that.

"Actually, ten thousand."

"Ten! Te! T!" I stammered. "Look here, old man, I wasn't thinking of putting that much into it. I thought I'd underwrite a few tubes of greasepaint. Or a couple of palm trees. That's all."

"But, Reggie, you have to help me. We were at school together."

There is no appeal more solemn than that. Woody had touched on the very code by which our family has lived for generations. The Rule of the Brubakers: Never turn down a friend in need. It pained me to have to decline.

"I simply don't have that much money at my disposal," I said. "It's all tied up. And back home in London." My ready stuff wasn't that ready.

Woody said, "Fine. Don't invest. Just loan me the money. No need for you to bankroll what's sure to be a multi-year run plus a touring company. I just need it for a couple of days."

He didn't seem to grasp that I didn't have access to that sort of kale, whether for a week or a twelvemonth.

Woody continued. "Today is October thirtieth. We open on November first. Everyone needs to be paid then. Between effusive newspaper reviews and word of mouth from ecstatic first-nighters, come November second, we'll have to beat would-be ticket buyers away with sticks."

"Are you certain?"

"I guarantee they'll be lined up from the box office all the way to Grant's Tomb. You'll get your money back that day."

"I'd like to help you, Woody. But on such short notice, I couldn't access even a fraction of that."

"Damn."

"Haven't you got a rich uncle or aunt you could appeal to?"

"Where do you think I got the king's ransom I've already sunk into this?"

"Any friends? Aren't all Americans millionaires? Seems like all the ones I meet are."

"That's because you stay at the Waldorf-Astoria, only eat at Twenty-One, and go to the races at Belmont Park. I really need this, Reggie. Otherwise—" He lowered his voice as a particularly beefy fellow hissed, "Move it, Buddy" and plowed through us, carrying enough lumber to build a small house. "I'll be in a lot of trouble. And worst of all, Kitty will leave me. She only agreed to marry me after I got her on the stage. She said it was a sign of my seriousness. What about *your* millionaire pals?"

"Sorry, Woody, I don't think I'm in a position to touch anyone for *ten thousand* of the best."

"Well, that's it then. I guess I'll go throw myself off the Brooklyn Bridge." He sighed. "There will be one less Old One at the next class reunion. Give my regards to Cloudy and Bongo." He turned away from me and started walking.

"Wait!" I cried.

Woody stopped.

"The Brooklyn Bridge is that way," I said, pointing left. "But there's no need to shuffle off your mortal coil. I have a solution."

"You do?"

"But of course. James."

~*~

We were in my hotel suite. Lovely rooms. Very art deco with lots of mirrors and parallel lines. I was in a white armchair while Woody reclined on a black sofa. The sun being over the yardarm, I was enjoying a whisky and soda while Woody sipped a martini. That's a lovely thing about the United States: even folks who never take a drink before noon can start five hours earlier owning to the different time zone.

We'd laid out the circumstances to James. He was not drinking. He stood at a sort of parade rest, as if he'd been given permission by his colonel to be at ease, but couldn't quite make himself do it. To be a valet is to be a creature of dignity.

"Indeed," James said. Which is what he frequently says while thinking.

"Take your time, James," I said. Even if I wasn't able to help Woody directly, I took comfort in the idea that James would. Vicarious assistance is not against the Rule of the Brubakers.

"Not too long," said Woody.

"One moment, please, gentlemen," James said, turning and slowly walking towards the suite's kitchen.

"Has he got it?" asked Woody. "He is coming back, isn't he?"

I took another sip. "Do relax, dear Woody. All will be revealed eventually. Ours is not to reason why. James has never failed me in a crisis."

A brief rustling sound came from the kitchen, and James reappeared bearing a newspaper.

"This, gentlemen, is today's *New York Patriot-Herald*. On page three," he turned the large pages over, "you will find an advertisement which I believe will satisfactorily answer your requirements. I noticed it this morning as I was unwrapping the kippers."

He laid the paper out on the coffee table (steel and glass, etchings of panthers rampant). Woody and I leaned in to read. Then we leaned back; it still smelled vaguely of fish. At the top of the page, within a large box bedecked with images of pumpkins and black cats arching their backs, was the following text:

THE NEW YORK PATRIOT-HERALD
ANNOUNCES
ITS THIRD ANNUAL
HALLOWEEN
PUMPKIN CARVING CONTEST
FIRST PRIZE $10,000

I knew of Halloween, of course. Not that big a bash back home across the pond. We prefer Guy Fawkes Night, when we can set off fireworks and burn chaps in effigy.

I was agog. "Someone is offering ten thousand dollars for first place in a *pumpkin carving contest?*" I'd heard of America's streets being paved with gold, but this was beyond the pale.

James said, "It is a publicity stunt, sir. No doubt the newspaper's proprietors calculate that they will more than recoup the expense through increased circulation and advertising revenue."

Woody nodded. "You'd be surprised what pays these days. Take those dance marathon contests. I saw on a newsreel that the winners of one bunion derby went at it for over two thousand hours. And they pocketed three thousand dollars in prize money. If we had the time, I'd take up flagpole sitting. That's where the real money is."

"Let me see if I have this right," I said. "All we have to do is carve a face on a pumpkin—"

"They're 'jack-o-lanterns' out here," added Woody.

"—submit the balmy thing, and, if we win, these newspaper tycoons will give us ten thousand of the real thing, American?"

"Indeed, sir," said James.

"Remarkable." Beneath the ad's box were the fine print details, which I perused. "Says here we have to turn it in by three o'clock on Halloween. That's approximately twenty-four hours from now." I rubbed my hands together, invigorated at the prospect. "That's a lot of cabbage for a pumpkin."

~*~

I don't know if you've ever attempted to carve a pumpkin, but, if you have, you know that the process is an absolute test of endurance. The thick shell needs to be punctured, and that takes the brawny arms of a village blacksmith. Then the entrails (seeds and such) must be removed, which requires both the steady hand of a diamond cutter and the cool disinterest of a professional butcher.

We had obtained our pumpkin from a local fruit cart. I was elected to do the carving. While none of the three of us had any experience working in gourd as a medium, I at least had once won second place in a school art competition with a pastel sketch depicting the routing of the Spanish Armada.

I had finished and was giving the old J-O-L a final inspection when Woody arrived at two the next afternoon, Halloween.

"That's it?" he cried in dismay. "That's all you've done?" He starred goggle-eyed at the pumpkin à la Brubaker. "It's just two eyes and a nose—all identical triangles—and a jagged gash for a mouth!"

"Both my theme and style are classical," I said. "I have endeavoured to create the archetypal jack-o-lantern."

"You spent all night on *that*?"

"It took quite a while to…Um, James, what was it that Italian chap said about whacking away with chisels?"

James replied, "The artist Michelangelo, when asked how he had created his masterpiece, the marble statue of David, is reputed to have replied, 'I simply removed everything that was not David.'"

"That's it," I said.

"That's not it at all," said Woody. "If anything, what you did was the opposite." He sank down into the couch. "You're an idiot, Reggie, and you've ruined us. Oh, Kitty, my love, farewell!"

I was taken aback. I had worked hard and was proud of the results of my labour. True, it was not the image of Napoleon I had started out to carve, but art is a series of compromises. As some chappie said, "Art is never finished, only abandoned."

I said, "Is that any way to talk to the principal backer of *The Cat and the Hula*?"

"You haven't put a penny into the show."

"But I soon shall. Have no fear, Woody. I guarantee this will be a winner. After all," I stepped over to him and put an arm around his shoulder, "the show must go on!"

Woody buried his face in his hands. "I'm ruined. There won't be any show. No one will work without being paid. And the crew will probably tear me limb from limb. They've all been promised money first thing tomorrow."

"James," I said, "what do you think of my pumpkin?"

"I have no doubt that in a contest whose stakes run to the five figures, it will be unique."

"Meaning," said Woody, "everyone else's will be *good*."

"James," I said, "pack this up in a hat box or a cake box or something. Then we're off to the offices of the *New York Patriot-Herald*."

"It's junk," muttered Woody.

"You clearly know nothing of art," I said. "We shall face this contest's judges with all the bravery of an early martyr facing a lion in the Roman Colosseum."

"Just before he gets eaten, you mean."

~*~

"Are you kiddin'?"

The man performing jack-o-lantern triage at the newspaper's front desk looked down upon my offering with scorn. "This ain't no kiddie show, pal. Only serious pumpkins make it to the judges." The lobby was crowded with people, young and old, armed with gourds of all shapes and sizes, their faces (the pumpkins', not the artists') carved in an amazing variety of visages from the gruesome to the comic.

"Next!" The man waved me to one side and examined the proffered pumpkin of the lady behind me. "OK, sister, yours will do." Her jack-o-lantern bore an amazing resemblance to the film star Edward G. Robinson, complete with pumpkin-stem cigar. He took her pumpkin, then asked her name and wrote it on a slip of paper. "Come back at six o'clock tonight. Sixth floor. That's when we'll have the judging." He turned away from her. "Next! No shoving, folks! No shoving!"

I tucked my pumpkin under my arm and walked back to Woody and James, who stood near a row of a dozen pay phone booths. "The man's a philistine," I said. "Does no one recognise true art anymore? Whatever happened to the spirit of *Arse Gratia Arse*?"

James coughed. "I believe, sir, you mean *Ars Gratia Artis*. Latin for 'Art for art's sake.' One pronounces the first word with the Voiced S."

"That's the ticket," I said.

"Is the Brooklyn Bridge to the left or the right of us?" asked Woody, slapping on his fedora.

"Your Lordship," said James to Woody, "need not take any drastic steps. I believe we are still in the running, so to speak."

"How so, James?" asked Woody, with exasperation. "They won't even let us on the track, so to speak."

"As it happens, I am on good terms with young Melvin Simms, the elevator operator in this building."

"Hold the phone," I said. "We've only been here three days. Until yesterday, you'd never even heard of this place."

"I took the opportunity while you were engaged in the exercise of your craft last night to familiarize myself with the environment where the contest is to take place."

"You cased the joint," I said.

"As you say, sir."

Woody asked, "What's this Melvin bloke going to do for us?"

"For a small gratuity, he should be able to take us to the sixth floor, and, more importantly, grant us access to the room where the contest finalists are being stored prior to the judges' arrival."

~*~

And so, just a couple of hours and a light dinner of lobster thermidor later, we three were standing in what is, in the parlance of the fourth estate, known as the newspaper's "morgue." It is the room in a newspaper office where past copies of said newspaper are kept. The archives, if you will. There were stacks and stacks of back issues dating to before Washington felled his first cherry tree.

Melvin had told us that the judges would be arriving in fifteen minutes. We could do whatever we wanted, but had to be out by 5:55. One large wooden desk had been cleared of half a year's worth of papers to make room for seven jack-o-lanterns.

Exactly what tactic to employ had been discussed over dinner. I had drawn the line at out-and-out cheating. A Brubaker has integrity, after all. Thus, we would not A) put my name and address on all of the identification tags. Nor would we B) steal all of the other contestant pumpkins. Likewise, there would be no C) disfiguring of the OCPs. Our plan was simply to circumvent—if that is the word I want—the irrational prejudice and lack of artistic sensibilities of the lobby gatekeeper, and to present to a candid world my creation in all its elegant simplicity.

What might seem to be an elementary plan immediately hit a snag. Where precisely should we insert my pumpkin in the lineup? Woody favoured first, while James asserted that fourth was the optimal locale, between a ghoulish, wrinkled jack-o-lantern with pointed ears and our old friend, the Edward G. Robinson pumpkin.

As the two debated the matter, I noticed the purple-covered script peeking out of a pocket of Woody's coat. Just to pass the time, I pulled the script from the pocket and started paging through it. I couldn't make any sense of it. The dialogue was mostly place names I was unfamiliar with, spelled with lots of accent marks in odd places. I came across what appeared to be a soliloquy. Absently, I began to recite, hoping that if I heard it out loud it would make more sense. After all, Shakespeare is like that.

As I spoke, the image of the Edward G. Robinson pumpkin kept running through my mind. The woman who had sculpted it had nailed that movie gangster's mug to a T.

I heard a moan.

I looked up from the script. Then I dropped it.

The EGR pumpkin was moving. Its thick, pumpkin rind lips slowly rolled the stem cigar from one side of its mouth to the other. Its eyes blinked.

"Mmm-yeah!" it moaned. Then again, more loudly. "Mmm-yeah, see!" Its eyes darted about, taking in the view. Being disembodied, the gourd could not move. But its parts could. Mouth, eyes, nose, and, I could now see, eyebrows, were fully animated.

Woody stood paralyzed.

"Indeed," said James. To be a valet is to be a creature of dignity.

"Who're you goons?" the pumpkin asked, his voice high and gravelly, remarkably like Robinson's in *Little Caesar*. Despite having no teeth to clench it, the stem-cigar now stayed in one place.

"Uh," said Woody.

I stepped towards the pumpkin, "Reginald Brubaker, at your service. This is my man James, and Fortescue, the Viscount Woodson." I spoke distinctly and without hesitation. Woody and I may have gone to the same schools, but breeding will out. We Brubakers have been in Britain since the time of the Conqueror.

"Mmm-yeah. Well, look here, see. I'm the Pumpkin. *The* Pumpkin. The Boss Pumpkin, see. The Great One like." His—I now had to think of him as a him—eyebrows arched and he frowned. His eyes were just

23

empty sockets, but they changed shape as he looked around. I could see the concave inside of his shell opposite the sockets, and, as the eyes moved, my view of that interior likewise shifted disconcertingly.

"On this night," he continued, "I rule all vegetation. Turnips cower before me, see. Carrots are my vassals. Mmm-yeah. All do my will!"

"Pleased to meet you," I said.

"Likewise," said Woody.

James inclined his head elegantly.

The Boss Pumpkin's eyes scurried across the surface of his pumpkin head like mice running on a globe. The head didn't move. Just the eyes. The inherent unnaturalness of this action made me feel a little dizzy.

"Dis ain't da place," he said. "Nah, see. Nah."

"Precisely what place do you mean, sir?" asked James.

"The patch, see. Mmm-yeah, the patch! Dat dizzy dame musta taken me out of mine. I gotta get to a patch, see." He spoke with a voice of authority that made me want to help him. This pumpkin was truly one of nature's noblemen. Like Edward G. Robinson, what he lacked in stature he made up for in sheer charisma. Or maybe it was the hypnotic effect of those eyeless sockets. His mouth twitched with a snarl. "Patch!" he shouted. His orange countenance swelled and distorted. Parts of his shell puckered. Bumps rose on either side of his face where ears might have been (How had he heard us, anyway?). Green leaves and vine sprouts quickly formed. "Not much time, see."

A Brubaker does not hesitate. I grabbed the Boss, Woody grabbed my experiment in Neo-Euclideanism, and James opened the morgue's door.

"Window," grunted the Boss, and we three rushed down the hallway towards a window. "So little time!

Faster!" Robinson qua pumpkin seemed much heavier than my own gourd and grew heavier with each step. We passed Melvin.

"Almost time for the—Oh, hey!" Melvin said. "Where you going?"

"Got to see a man about a horse," I shouted.

"Did you say *hearse?*" asked Melvin.

"Quite possibly," yelled Woody over his shoulder.

James tipped his bowler hat and followed.

"Thanks for the five-spot!" shouted Melvin, waving the lettuce and heading back to the elevator.

We stopped at the nearest window. It was two feet across by three feet high, hardly big enough for any of us to pass through. Not that we'd want to, six floors up.

"Now what?" I asked.

The Boss Pumpkin proclaimed, "I am The Pumpkin! Do my bidding!"

The window began to shake. Through the glass, I could see ivy moving. It gripped the glass of the window and its frame. Then, with a tremendous rip, the window was gone, falling through the air to eventually shatter six stories below. I could see the lights of Manhattan and the stars above.

"Now what?" I asked the Boss.

"BEHOLD!" he proclaimed, and thick, kelly-green tendrils shot out from his spherical phiz. Some grew to resemble giant, leafy wings. Still others wrapped themselves around our waists. "Onward, see!" he yelled. I had to drop him since he had become too awkward to handle, and, frankly, too large. He was now almost the size of a St. Bernard dog. Though I knew there was no candle inside him, he glowed luminously.

Using his vines as limbs to gain leverage, The Boss flung himself out the window, dragging us with him.

~*~

I don't know if you've ever flown over New York City, carried by a giant pumpkin that was propelling itself with wings. If you have, then you know the combination of terror and exhilaration that filled me. It was rather like being at the top of a Ferris wheel when it stops. All of the city is laid out before you—the millions of lives, the millions of stories—but you really can't enjoy it as much as you'd like because you feel as if you're about to crash to your death at any moment.

"I need a patch!" the Boss yelled. His huge mouth (originally the size of a small banana, now a watermelon) had swung around to the back of his head to talk to us while his eyes remained straight ahead. "I don't see nuthin'. Just apartments and offices. So much iron and steel and cement. I need a patch! Dat dame! Aargh! The sun is already down!"

We three were suspended below the Boss (who was now the size of a horse) by thick tendrils. Their ends girdled us around our chests, below our arms, like steamship life preservers. Woody had lost his fedora but still held my own small gourd. Despite the wind generated by the Boss's speed blowing through us and around us, James's bowler remained firmly in place. The man is remarkable.

"I believe I can offer a solution," said James.

"You can?" I asked. I had to shout to be heard against the rushing wind. "When did you have time to learn the location of all the pumpkin patches in Manhattan?"

The Boss said, "Mmm-yeah. If you got a answer, Buddy, I'm all ears."

"Markedly not," said James. "But, nonetheless. If you will turn left at the next block and then travel up Fifth Avenue, a satisfactory solution will present itself."

"Okay, pal." The mouth swung back to the front of the Boss's face.

Woody said, "I know that area. That's—"

"Indeed, it is, Your Lordship."

"That's not a pumpkin patch."

"Indeed, it is not."

~*~

The sun had set, but New York City is never entirely in darkness. Lights everywhere illuminated the skyscrapers and townhouses. Light picked out for us the outlines of buildings, if not the buildings themselves. And it framed the many square miles of darkness that lay at the heart of Manhattan. Lights ran along 59th Street to Fifth Avenue to 110th Street, then back down again.

Though its lush, green lawns and trees were mere shadows, light framed Central Park.

"That spot to the left might be propitious," James said. "It looks particularly abandoned."

The Boss Pumpkin's giant green wings shifted, and we slowly descended.

After a few moments, he set us down with surprising care. We were in one of the Park's many shaded glens. We were alone.

The Boss propped himself up on legs of vines that hung from his base like braces ("suspenders" at Brooks Brothers) that had fallen off the shoulders of a very fat man dressed all in orange. His eyes, as large as dinner plates, circumnavigated his head, causing me more dizziness, then came to rest facing us.

"What gives? Dis ain't no patch, see," he said to James. "I need a patch to *move*. I need a patch to launch! Sure, I can fly through part of one city, see. But to spread the spirit, I need a patch to charge me up! I need power to launch. I gotta get everywhere, see. Without me there is no Halloween!"

"Have no fear. It was Mr. Brubaker who brought you to life. He is a powerful wizard."

"He is?" asked Woody, setting down my pumpkin.

"He is," said James. Then, to the Boss, he said, "He can give you the energy you need to embark on your journeys."

"He can?" asked Woody.

"He can," said James.

"Mmm-yeah, well then, do it, see," said the Boss.

I looked at James. What was I supposed to do? I was no wizard. I didn't own a pointy hat or wand. Even my embroidered dressing gown at home featured sheep, not astrological symbols. I shrugged.

"Come on!" snarled the Boss Pumpkin.

James said, "Perhaps, sir, the spell as it was cast at the Drury Lane Theatre last Christmas."

Ah! I raised my arms above my head like the evil wizard in the comedic Christmas panto production of *Aladdin* I'd seen almost a year earlier. I had no memory of the magic words he'd used, so I said the first thing that came into my head:

> *Oh, Boss Pumpkin*
> *You must go*
> *To spread your spirit*
> *To and fro*
> *Oh, Boss Pumpkin*
> *Don't be late*
> *Fly forth and be*
> *The gourd so great*

"Your poems are right up there with your sculptures," muttered Woody.

I looked at the Boss Pumpkin. Now what? I had done what James has suggested, but I had no idea what it was supposed to accomplish.

Suddenly, the Boss's eyes grew wider and he moaned, "Mmm-yeah!" His mouth twisted from a frown into a rictus grin. "Yes!" he shouted. "Now I feel it. I am connected. I feel the charge, see! Oh, this is the ultimate patch. I feel myself all the way to them Pyramids and over to Stonehenge. And way down under to Ayers Rock. I have the power. Halloween has come!" His huge bulk glided silently on tendrils towards me. "You, Wizard Brubaker. How can I repay you?"

What did a pumpkin have that I would I want? Even unto half his kingdom is still just a bunch of seeds.

"We could use ten grand," piped up Woody.

The Boss squinted. "Do you mean money?"

I nodded enthusiastically.

James said, "Not everyone can live on water and photosynthesis."

"Oh, but of course," said the Boss. He gave the smallest flick of a vine, and my pumpkin turned into a pile of cash.

Woody gasped, then dropped to the pile, drew out a bill, and held it up to the moonlight. "A hundred-dollar bill," he said. "It looks real." He held it to his nose. "It smells real." He licked it. "Tastes real."

"Farewell, see," the Boss said. "Wizard Brubaker and...strange company."

And without so much as laying a tendril aside of his nose, he ascended. Higher and higher he rose until he was out of sight.

"There's something you don't see every day," said Woody. He waved another greenback from the pile. "Our worries are over. Well done, Reggie. Well done, James."

"James," I said, "what is that word you use when you mean to say 'clear things up'?"

"'Elucidation,' sir?"

"Yes. I'm going to need a dashed lot of elucidation."

"Of course, sir. Of the exact nature and purpose of the Boss Pumpkin, I could not hazard a guess. However, based on what he said, I believe he would have come to life in his own pumpkin patch, had he been left there. That is his natural state and function. Outside of a patch, he would not have. Perhaps, just as a caterpillar turning into a butterfly requires the specific environment of a cocoon, he requires a pumpkin patch. We will never know."

I asked, "How did he come to life then? You said I did it."

"I believe you were perusing the script of the show at that time, sir?"

"Yes."

"It is a singular script. I read it at my table in the back of the restaurant while you gentlemen were developing your plan. I believe you brought the Boss to life through speaking a spell that was accidentally or intentionally embedded in the text."

"But," said Woody, "we've had weeks of rehearsals and nothing like that has ever happened before."

I said, "Ah! But you'd never had a pumpkin in the audience before."

"A shrewd observation, sir," said James. "Also, I believe the fact that it is Halloween contributed to, let us say, the availability of magic."

"It was in the air, eh," I said.

"Indeed, sir."

Woody said, "So we need to make sure not to sell any tickets to pumpkins, and maybe we should go dark every Halloween. Got it. Thanks, James."

"My pleasure, Your Lordship."

"But what was all that launching stuff?" I asked. "And the bit about power? He said he needed to be in a patch to launch. This is not a patch."

"I have an aunt who is an avid gardener. It has long been a maxim of hers that all pumpkin patches are connected through ley lines."

"Through what?" I asked.

"Oh," said Woody, "I've heard of those. They're sort of like the power cables that bring electricity to our houses. But they're made of spectral aether or something. And they deliver magic."

"A close enough approximation," said James. "I deduced that it was these that power the Boss Pumpkin's travels. He just needed a few minutes to tap into them."

I said, "That may be so, but this is still not a pumpkin patch."

"Indeed not, sir. But Central Park is nonetheless a major ley line confluence. A hub, so to speak, of such magic powers."

"And how exactly did you learn that?"

"The aunt in question emigrated to the United States many years ago, and her subsequent letters to me have contained a wide variety of notes of interest."

"Ah, I get it. She emigrated to New York City. She's up on all the local gourd gossip."

"No, sir. She moved to Salem, Massachusetts. But she travels widely."

"James, I will never question your sources again. It's best to accept that you are a singular fellow."

"Thank you, sir."

"But where did the money come from?" asked Woody. He was nearly done stuffing his coat pockets with the cash.

I said, "I think I've got this one, James." I turned to Woody, "You heard it from his own lips. On this night, he controls the vegetable kingdom."

"Oh, no," said Woody. You don't mean—"

"Yes, he commands all the cabbage, kale, and lettuce. In fact, all the green stuff in the world."

"Amazing," said Woody.

James said, "How right you are, sir."

I said, "Let us see if we can find a horse-drawn cab anywhere in this park. I, for one, could use a stiff whisky and soda."

Woody said, "Hold on a sec. I need to adjust...There's something in it. Hmm. Wonder how that got there."

"What?"

"In my shoe. Somehow...I got a rock."

For Sparky

~*~

The Real Estate Market
Lara Frater

~*~

Great Deal Spacious 5 Bd, 3 ½ ba House In Dix Hills. Nice Quiet Neighborhood, Good Schools, Near RR. LR, DR, Den, Family Room, Fireplaces, Fully Finished basement, Pool, Large Yard, Two Car Garage! Great Condition. Ready To Move In! Affordable! Reduced Price And Negotiable! Must Sell ASAP. Contact Red River Realty.

"Lisa, look at this." My wife stood by the stove where she had been cleaning up. She walked towards me and kicked a matchbox car across the room. The toy made a light bang as it hit the wall.

"Bobby!" she yelled at my son who was playing with other toys in the living room. "I told you not to play with these in the kitchen!" She had been moody since entering her second trimester of pregnancy. It didn't help that our daughter Taffy was still pretty much a baby herself. We had been searching for a house that fit our family for six months with no luck.

"Sorry, mom." He went back to his toys. He would forget this after about five minutes. Thankfully her yelling didn't wake up our daughter who was asleep in the next room.

I looked at our living room where my oldest—6-year-old Bobby—played. The entire living room was shelving units filled with kid's toys. Cars, trucks, and robots for Bobby, stuffed animals for Taffy. Our things were shoved into ceiling-high crates in the corner. The kid's room was barely big enough to hold the two of them let alone their toys. We gave them the master bedroom to share while we took the smaller kid's room as our own. Seven months ago, I had gotten a huge promotion at the investment firm I worked at. Lisa and I had saved for a down payment that our folks helped fatten, and we were now at the point we could buy a decent three-bedroom house.

She picked up the *Times* and read the ad. "We can't afford it. Honey, there's no way a house in Dix Hills could be affordable unless there's something wrong with it. It's one of those crazy ads or a bait and switch."

I figured she was right, but I thought it might be worth the effort. I grabbed my cell. "I'm gonna call them. It's been six months and we've found nothing."

My wife looked over the ad again and shrugged her shoulders. She didn't look convinced.

The real estate agent Pam agreed to meet us next Saturday morning at the house. My jaw dropped when she told me the price. It wasn't just in our price range; it was lower than what we wanted to spend. Pam assured me it was actually in Dix Hills, that the property was in good condition, and zoned for all the area schools.

I got my folks to watch the kids. I expected the house to be dilapidated with paper thin walls that were put up later to make up the tiny bedrooms. I really didn't think it was in Dix Hills. It was probably in Wheatley Heights. The pool wouldn't be in ground, it would be one of those ugly, blow up ones, and the yard would be the size of a postage stamp. I was sure it wasn't "ready to move in."

"Oh my god!" my wife said when we pulled up in front of it. I felt the same way. Not only were we in Dix Hills proper, this house was bigger than any house in our price range. It was a huge light red brick-faced Colonial with no signs of cracked paint. It had three stories with a slanted roof and a chimney.

The house wasn't next to a rendering plant and there was a decent amount of space between us and our neighbors. It was weird, but it smelled faintly of beef. I guess someone was having a barbeque even though it was fall. Not a bad smell. If we ever got a house, I looked forward to firing up the grill in the summer.

The neighboring houses were also gorgeous and of similar size and shape. The street was quiet except for a gardener working on some bushes on a neighboring house. I caught his eye and he made the sign of the cross before he went back to his work.

Ignoring his odd behavior, I turned back to Lisa. I assumed the woman in front of the house was Pam because she wore a red blazer with a big name tag that read *My name is Pam!*

"Hello!" She put on the fakest smile I'd ever seen. I figured it must be tiring to smile like that all day. "You must be Mr. and Mrs. Tanner. I'm Pam from Red River Realty. Glad you could stop by."

"This place is gorgeous." My wife still looked stunned. "And please, call me Lisa."

"Wait until you see inside, you'll love it." Pam led us past an iron gate with an enormous lock. The gate was open and we walked about twenty steps to a covered porch that had a shiny crystal light fixture above it. Around the walkway was a large front yard.

Pam opened a door that led to a foyer with polished wood floors. Past the foyer, to the left, a staircase led up to the second floor. To my right, a huge sitting room held a fireplace. Next to the sitting room, a giant living room with wood floors looked like the perfect place for entertaining guests. Directly in front of us was a long hallway. I rubbed my finger on the staircase. Not a hint of dust. I smelled the air. All I could smell was beef. I was ready to barbeque right now, whatever season.

"Come this way."

We passed the staircase. There was a closet underneath. I wasn't a contractor but so far, I couldn't see any flaws. I reached out to touch the knob.

Before I could, Pam grabbed my hand. "It's just a big closet."

"Let's see it." I expected mold, which I knew was hard to get rid of. I didn't want my children in a mold-filled house.

Pam smiled her big fake rosy smile and opened the door. It was a huge closet; big enough to be a room. The beef smell was stronger here and there appeared to be brown paint all over the wall, but not a hint of mold or mildew.

"Sorry, we're still doing some painting." Pam slammed the door.

I hadn't smelled paint.

Next to the closet was another door. "Here's the basement." This time she voluntarily opened the door. "We can look at that at the end of the tour."

That's it. The basement's got to be a swamp or a toxic waste dump. Except I didn't smell anything but beef. Some neighbor must have been having a massive party.

"Basement is full and finished. It has a family and rec room, a full-size bath, laundry room, and even space for an office." She led us past the hallway into a large dining room with a crystal chandelier in the center. There was a kitchen towards the back.

"Kitchen is very modern. I want to show you something lovely." We walked into a kitchen almost as big as my first apartment. In the back, a spiral staircase and a big picture window made for a nice focal point.

A huge backyard held an in-ground pool covered in plastic. Lush evergreen trees and multiple colored oak and maple trees surrounded the yard. It made the backyard kind of forest like. It was a beautiful sight. I never imagined owning a house like this. Lisa and I figured we might be able to get a three bedroom, one and half bath in a nice upper- to middle-class neighborhood.

"The yard covers an entire acre. The pool needs to be cleaned and filled, but it is structurally sound. I can recommend a good pool company. This stairwell and the one in the front go up to the second and third floors." She climbed as we followed.

We got to the second floor and were yet again greeted by polished wooden floors and a big picture window through which I could see the picturesque yard and pool. The floor made no signs of creaking or loose or rotted wood.

"Three bedrooms and one full bath on this floor. And there are two bedrooms on the third floor, although it used to be three. The previous owners made their master bedroom into a suite and put in a Jacuzzi—"

"All right!" I'd had enough. Pam and Lisa looked startled, but I didn't care. "This is too good to be true. What the hell is wrong with this house?"

"Rob, don't be rude."

"No, Lisa, I can't help it. This house is amazing. There is nothing wrong with it. But there has to be."

"I assure you that there is nothing wrong with this house. It's been checked by contractors. Obviously, you can have your own come in during escrow." Pam didn't lose her cheery demeanor.

"Come on, Pam. You know something's wrong here. If I go next door I bet they'll tell me they paid a couple of mil for their house."

Pam's eternal smile became a frown. "Come this way."

We followed her down the spiral staircase into the massive kitchen. The kitchen had a large combo fridge and freezer, but it also had a large chest freezer next to it. She opened the freezer and pulled out what looked like a roast wrapped in plastic.

"Pam—" I said, confused. Now nothing made sense.

"You wanted to see what was wrong. I'm going to show you what's wrong. I was going to wait until the end of the tour."

We followed her to the front of the house to the staircase we first saw when we entered. At the second floor, we met a weird sight: between the second and third floor was another door five feet behind a railing.

Strange looking, but it looked like someone added an extra closet. Pam jumped over.

I followed and we both helped Lisa.

So, the house had a weird mezzanine that might bring the value down. Certainly not down to our price range. This area smelled especially strongly of beef, and it wasn't coming from Pam's roast.

Pam pulled out a key from her pocket, unwrapped the meat, and then unlocked and opened the door.

An intense wind came out of the closest with a roar. Inside the closet looked like it was filled with thousands of strobe lights. Among the roar of the wind, I could hear a humming, then a low growl, finally a screaming voice.

"Meat!"

Pam threw the chuck into the closet. The action happened quickly, but I couldn't hear the roast hit the floor before Pam slammed the door.

"What the fuck was that?" Lisa looked bewildered. I looked back at the closed closet door and reached for the handle, buy Pam slapped my hand away.

"Don't open the door unless you have to. Otherwise, it gets greedy and demanding, and you'll have to feed it more often and with more than just meat—if you catch my drift." She pulled the key out and locked the door.

"I don't understand," Lisa still looked bewildered. "What's that?"

"We don't know what's in there and no one's tried to find out. Although there are rumors someone tried a long time ago. As you can hear, it wants meat. I've been feeding it for the last couple of months. It needs a couple pounds of beef once a week and there won't be any trouble. It can be cheap meat. I know a place that sells it wholesale."

"That's it?" Pam looked at me, confused.

"Well—Even though the door is locked, occasionally it opens, screams, and blood comes pouring out. It's done that every time I showed the house—" She paused. "But not with you. Why, it's been quiet this whole time. It must like you."

"And the brown paint in downstairs closet? Dried blood?"

She nodded. "It leaks sometimes. You'll have to keep that closet empty."

"What happened to the previous owners?"

Pam didn't respond.

"Come on, Pam, you've already told us almost everything."

"The last couple lived here fifty years with no trouble. I think they got senile and forgot to feed it. They never found the bodies. The daughter originally rented out the house, but none of the tenants could live with having to feed this thing and the screaming and cleaning up the blood."

"Foundation is strong, no leaks, warm in winter, cool in summer? No radon, not on the national priority list for cleanup?" I asked.

"Yes, and I'll be happy to have your contractor come in and test the rest of the place. You aren't going to find a nicer house than this one at such a deeply discounted price in such a wonderful neighborhood. I have a list of people who can work on the house and are familiar with the issue."

"All we have to do is buy meat and throw it into the closet? Which occasionally spits blood and screams—but that's it?"

"Yes."

"How come you haven't been able to sell the house in the past? I'm sure someone would still buy it despite this closet."

"Oh, there were some unsavory individuals who expressed interest and some others that really didn't fit into the neighborhood's lifestyle. We really would like to keep the neighborhood nice. You seem like a good family," she looked at the closet. "It seems to like you. It probably knows you'll take care of this house. Come on," Pam's fake rosy smile returned. "It's very inexpensive for such a small inconvenience."

I looked at my wife. I thought about the entire family squashed in a two-bedroom apartment, then thought about us relaxing by the pool. I thought about the cost of the higher taxes, meat once a week, the cost of putting up walls around the closet to keep the kids out. We might be house poor until Lisa went back to work, but I think we could manage it. We'd have to find someone willing to throw the meat in when we went on vacation. We could always sell the house when we get older or if the thing in the closet became too much of a nuisance.

"What do you think Lisa?"

"We'll take it."

~*~

Mirror, Mirror

Peter Cawdron

~*~

Monsters & Machines

JENNY PEERS OUT from beneath her duvet, whispering, "Are the monsters coming for us? For me?" She feels a little silly, somewhat paranoid for asking, but given what she's heard, she has to know.

"I won't let them hurt you," her mother says, sitting on the edge of her bed.

Even though Susan Culpepper is a slight figure, the aging mattress sags beneath her weight. The light bulb strung from the ceiling waxes and wanes, pulsating with the irregular electrical supply. After four years of war, the civil infrastructure upon which society depends is crumbling like the buildings above them. Explosions rock the surface. Walls collapse, falling in the street as the battle rages overhead.

Basement parking lots like these have become bomb shelters, protecting humans during the dark of night when monsters prowl. Susan Culpepper tucks her daughter in, tightening the bedsheets around the girl's petite frame, swaddling her, wanting to make her feel secure.

"We will rise again," she says, kissing Jenny on the forehead. "Get some sleep."

"Yes, Mom." But Jenny can't sleep. Like most teens, she's deprived of any real rest by the war, sleeping in fits and waking in a start. If it's not gunfire and explosions ravaging her dreams, it's the uneasy still of night. On those rare occasions when the fighting stops, she's terrified to think why. *Has the night guard been overrun? Are monsters quietly slipping between their beds, slitting the throats of children in their sleep, damning them to never wake?*

Susan Culpepper joins several other parents over by the exit ramp. The bunker is three stories down, but moonlight still drifts through the shattered floors above. The adults talk in hushed tones. Those children sleeping near them hear, and pass messages in a whisper to those too far away for sound to travel. From where she is, Jenny catches snippets of the conversation, just those few words that echo within the concrete basement, drifting between explosions and the ricochet of bullets outside.

"The shelter on Maple St. was overrun. They surrendered. It was that or die."

"They should have died," Susan says, a little too loudly for the quiet of night. "This is our planet. Our home. I will not surrender our way of life. We have to hold onto our past or there's no future for our children."

A murmur of agreement echoes between the adults, but Jenny doesn't catch any of the replies. She wants to fall asleep, but she can't. A shadow appears beside her bed. Deon smiles from the darkness. Somehow, he's crawled through the suitcases and backpacks, squeezing beneath her bed and into the aisle.

"Shhhh," he says. "Are you coming?"

"The lights are still on," Jenny says, but the lights are a soft yellow, feeble in their attempt to fight off the darkness. No one's been able to read anything beneath them for years. They're a good alternative to the pitch black of the basement, but no good for anything else. As if on cue, the lights start turning off from the far end of the parking lot, slowly reaching them. This pseudo-night is supposed to help the kids sleep, but it terrifies most of them. Within a minute, there are only a few guide lights still running, just enough for the adults to move around when checking on their kids.

"You're crazy," Jenny says.

"We all are," Deon replies.

Jenny is thirteen. She remembers when the conquest began. At first, it was peaceful. Flying saucers defying gravity, spinning slowly as they hovered over cities and farmland. She never saw one herself, but they were all that was ever on the news. Six ships. One for each inhabited continent and the surrounding islands. Six ships covering eight billion souls on one tiny planet.

Initially, there were calls for resistance, calls to fight the invaders, but the extremists were largely ignored. Scientists, astronomers, and astronauts embraced the aliens because they shared the secrets of the universe, teaching how to detect and even manipulate both dark matter and dark energy. Philosophers said it was the end of human history, that life on Earth would never be the same again. They were more right than they knew. Politicians rallied the public to embrace a new age.

The aliens initiated a renaissance in medical science, wiping out dozens of diseases overnight, but no one ever saw them. The only images that made it on television were of machines. They weren't robots, mimicking some humanoid form. Instead, there were an array of widely different industrial robotic body types, all with a specialized purpose. Most of them looked like the arms on an auto assembly line. Gene sequencers were square blocks about the size of a fridge, while the printers were the size of a house and able to build entire houses—complete with wiring and plumbing—in less than a day. Driverless cars were replaced with driverless flyers. They looked similar to the UFOs but with vast hollow centers containing fans that worked like the blades of a helicopter.

The only tech the aliens wouldn't give humanity was that of interstellar spaceflight. They said we weren't ready. At the time, no one paid too much attention to what they may have meant by that, as there were so many other toys to play with. It seemed as though that was being saved for Christmas. Then the change happened.

At first, it was in the Middle East. Angry young men, radicalized in their hatred of each other because they disagreed over ancient scrolls, suddenly became friends and began helping each other. Jenny didn't understand why that was so bad. Friends are good. Deon and Jenny are friends. Her Mom said it was evil.

Most civilized countries didn't care. Backwater nations were being dragged into the present. Women's rights. Education. Reproductive freedom. Equality. Who would oppose these movements arising in Afghanistan or Qatar? But when machines were found in Texas and Arkansas, and people began changing their attitudes without coercion, Americans freaked out. Suddenly, everyone was nice, and the authorities knew this was wrong. The arrival of the aliens had turned into an invasion, a not-so-hostile takeover enslaving the planet, or so they said on the news.

Jenny's mom said the problem was that the aliens took away free will. Humans had a God-given right to be knuckleheads, and that was being stripped from them by creatures from another world. No one oppresses humans—that job is reserved for humans alone. But worse than that, the oppressed were happy, relieved. They were deluded. Deceived. Conquered without any shots fired.

What's next? That was the question that preoccupied the adults. Was humanity to become Soylent Green? Food for alien hordes waiting in space? Did anyone really believe there were just six ships and not an armada poised to attack the planet? *Homo sapiens* domesticated chickens, pigs, and cows, taming them and separating them from their wild counterparts for one reason: so they could eat them. Is that what the aliens were doing? Domesticating eight billion sheep?

Humanity wouldn't have it.

Six ships. Six targets. Six nuclear weapons. Five of them were launched from submarines hidden in the depths of the ocean. One was dropped by a bomber.

There were no shields or any kind of missile defense on the alien spacecraft. It was as though they never felt in danger from humanity.

The military was ready for a protracted battle, but that didn't happen either. At least, not at first. There were six strikes. Six decimated radioactive hulls lying crumpled on the landscape of six different cities. They never found the aliens, just more machines.

That short, brief war unified the planet. The world celebrated. Freedom had been won. Six months later, the first attacks began. It took some time for the military to realize they'd been infiltrated. They were fighting an enemy within. Those happy, cheerful, helpful, cured folk undertook an insurrection. The remaining alien machines banded together with them, and the major cities were reduced to rubble.

No one's sure where all the weapons came from, as there seems to be no end to the destruction. Deon told Jenny that before the aliens even arrived, there were enough bombs and guns and stuff to kill everyone on the planet several times over. From what Jenny's seen, that seems to be the general plan.

"They found something up there."

"What?" Jenny asks.

"A machine. A dead machine. You want to see it?"

Jenny's quiet.

"You're scared."

"I'm not scared." Jenny doesn't actually answer his question. Bravado beats honesty. She never wants to go topside, even during the day, but she feels compelled to face her fears. That's the only way she can find peace.

She pulls at the sheets, slipping out of bed and into the walkway between the bunks. Most of the other kids are asleep. Those that aren't watch in silent admiration, wishing they were as brave. Jenny grabs her winter coat from beneath her bunk and shoves it in her bed, along with a pair of boots. She pushes at them until the shape they form is vaguely reminiscent of someone curled up beneath the covers. Jenny is particular, pulling the sheets tight and tucking them beneath the mattress. Her mom will check. Once her mom sees the sheets are still neatly in place, she'll sneak back to join the other adults for some moonshine as a nightcap.

"Come on."

Jenny slips on some shoes and creeps along behind Deon.

"Hey, where are you—"

"Shhh," Deon says to the darkness.

"I'm coming too." Lisa drops from an upper bunk, landing with the grace of a cat, barely making any sound. She doesn't bother with her bedding. Her mom isn't as paranoid as Jenny's. If her mom notices anything, she'll think Lisa has gone to the bathroom, or curled up with one of her friends. Lisa is impulsive. If she gets cold or scared, she'll do something about it. Last winter, Jenny woke squished against the side of her bunk, with Lisa snuggled in beside her to keep warm. Lisa blames her nocturnal behavior on sleepwalking, but whenever Jenny's seen her on the move, she's been very much awake. Like Jenny, Lisa doesn't like to admit when she's scared.

Lisa grabs some shoes, but doesn't put them on. She probably doesn't want to fall behind.

They creep past the bathrooms. The smell is pungent, which keeps the adults away. Most people try to hold it in until dawn and go topside, as the rats in the basement sewers are known to bite. A cockroach crunches under Jenny's shoes.

"Delightful," she says.

"What is?" Lisa asks, stepping on another roach, only she's still in bare feet.

"Never mind."

"Where are we going?" Lisa asks.

"The scouts found a 7-11," Deon says. "I bet there's still candy."

"Eww." All Jenny can imagine is ransacked shelves covered in fuzzy mold and rat droppings.

"The hard stuff, like mints and Jolly Ranchers, will still be good."

"I hope so," Lisa says.

"I'm not eating anything I can't soak in boiling water." Jenny's had enough of the basement trots, as stomachaches are called among the kids. She doesn't want to spend the next few nights darting between her bunk and the latrine a dozen times.

"And you're sure about the machine?" Lisa asks, wiping her feet on a dirty mat and slipping on her shoes.

"What about monsters?" Jenny asks.

"There are no monsters," Deon replies, which Jenny finds surprising—not that he's denying the existence of monsters, but that he chose to ignore Lisa's question. What if the machine isn't dead?

"How do you know there aren't any monsters?" Jenny asks, feeling defiant.

"Parents have always lied to their kids. The tooth fairy. Santa Claus. Rover going to doggy heaven. Haven't you ever wondered why?"

"Why, smartypants?" Lisa asks.

"Because lies are easy. Lies are simple. Lies avoid awkward questions."

"But why would they lie?" Jenny asks. "Why not just tell us the truth?"

Deon looks at her as though he's explaining trigonometry to a preschooler. "Telling lies has always been the easiest way to control people—kids *and* adults."

The children climb through the shattered remains of a stairwell. Starlight drifts down from above. A concrete slab has fallen from one of the upper floors, blocking the stairs. It's too big for an adult to squeeze past, but the kids have no problem pulling themselves through. They've gone this way dozens of times before, but they normally go up to the second floor where they can peer out over the devastated remains of the park and watch distant battles unfold like fireworks on the 4th of July.

For Jenny, defiance is like breathing. It's not that she's deliberately bad, or naughty, but being cooped up in the basement seems to squeeze the life out of her. She needs to breathe. Those damn bedsheets say one thing to her mother, but something else to her. Security or enslavement? Protection or prison?

It's dangerous being up top at night. The kids know they could be mistaken by both sides, but to see the stars is a reward in itself. They're beautiful—unmoved by a petty war on a puny planet.

"This way," Deon says, creeping through the shattered remains of the office tower. Once, this building was majestic. Vast open ceilings on the ground floor stretched up over twenty feet. Massive plate glass windows lined the lobby. Marble floors. Fancy furniture. Now, it's dusty and covered with fallen debris. Broken glass crunches softly beneath their shoes.

Deon freezes, holding a hand out in the moonlight, signaling for the girls to stop. Jenny's heart pounds in her chest. Soldiers walk past outside. They're crossing the road, relaxed as they talk with each other, their rifles shouldered. The kids creep over to a support pillar, hiding in the shadows.

"I'm not sure about this," Jenny says. This isn't as much fun as sneaking upstairs and watching the world outside. She feels exposed down on the ground.

"I want to go back," Lisa says.

"Me too."

Deon says, "Then go."

"You're leaving us?" Lisa asks in barely a whisper.

Deon points at the stairwell. "You're being chicken—chicken children."

"That's not fair," Jenny says. "We could die out there."

"You could die down there," Deon replies, pointing into the darkness. "That's what happened to the refugees on Maple Street."

"They lived," Jenny says. "Mom said so."

"Did she?" Deon asks. "Did she tell you what she thought *should* have happened to them?"

Lisa doesn't understand. "What?" she asks, looking at Jenny with innocent eyes.

"She thought they should have died."

"*Why?*" she asks. Exasperation hangs in the air between them.

Jenny shakes her head. As much as she loves her mom, she doesn't understand how her mom can think that way. "I—I don't know. She didn't mean it. I'm sure she didn't."

Lisa says, "I don't want to die."

Deon shakes his head. "I hate to spoil the party, but sooner or later, we all die. You know that, right? You can be afraid of dying, or you can live life to the full. You can't do both."

Jenny nods, but she's afraid of death. She doesn't want to admit that to herself, but Deon knows. It's not the thought of dying that terrifies her, it's that there's suddenly no tomorrow. The universe has been around for almost thirteen *billion* years, but not for her. To her mind, time has only existed for a mere thirteen years. Before then, there was nothing—not from her perspective. Afterwards, there will be nothing again. Nothing is scarier than any monster. When she wakes in the dark of night, with her heart racing and a cold sweat breaking out on her forehead, she wants for something, anything other than nothing.

"I heard about the kids beneath central station," she says softly, speaking as though she's uttering some dark incantation and in danger of waking the dead. "They found them with their throats slit."

"What kind of monster would do that?" Lisa asks.

Jenny shrugs. "I don't know."

"Makes you wonder, doesn't it?" Deon asks. "What we're up against? Why we're at war?"

Lisa is chirpy, recalling the reason they're constantly told by the adults. "Because we're fighting for freedom."

"That's not a reason," Deon says, peering out at the desolate street. "No one's ever free. There's always someone in control."

"We're fighting baddies," Jenny says. "Monsters."

"Shhh," Deon replies, crouching as a mechanized unit rolls through the intersection ahead. Spotlights flicker across the war-torn buildings. Lisa and Jenny crouch behind him. Within seconds, the armored personnel carrier has moved on.

In the distance, flashes of light set the dark buildings in silhouette as a battle rages a couple of miles away. The rumble of thunder rolls through the air, but there are no clouds in the sky.

"What are they looking for?" Jenny asks as the APC disappears around the corner.

"Machines," Deon replies.

"What do the machines want?" Jenny asks.

"Us."

Jenny doesn't like that answer. "Why would they want us?"

"That's a good question."

"You ask too many questions," Lisa says.

Deon smiles. "And you ask too few." He creeps into the moonlight. "Time to go."

A cat scurries away as they approach a burned-out restaurant, which is a good sign since cats steer clear of humans. Barbecued cat is a delicacy.

Deon sneaks through the forecourt of the plaza, ducking behind a park bench beside an empty fountain. The brass pipes and plastic lines once created a visual spectacle out of something as simple as water, but now they seem naked, strangely out of place.

Jenny takes a deep breath and darts out after Deon, with Lisa following close behind. She comes up beside him and peers over the edge of the fountain, crouching as she holds onto a concrete rim that once doubled as a bench seat.

"There had better not be any monsters," Jenny says.

Deon laughs.

She's not so sure. During the day, markets unfold in the shattered remains of the plaza. Crops are grown in the park. There's nothing scary about the forecourt in the daylight, but at night, the shadows are evil.

"This way."

They follow Deon behind the plaza, climbing over a low cinderblock wall and down to the riverbank. Masts of sunken boats protrude from the water at odd angles. Several yachts lie beached on the bank, with their cabins partially beneath the waterline.

Deon moves quickly.

Jenny's more cautious. The last thing she needs is mud on her clothing. Her mom will notice. As it is, she'll have to hide her shoes when she gets back to the basement.

"How far away is this place?"

"Not far," Deon says, leading them beneath a motorway overpass. The center of the bridge has been bombed, probably not for any strategic reason except that it was there. They climb around the rubble, avoiding crossing the top of the debris so their motion isn't easy to spot from a distance. Having lived in the ruins for years, they know all the tricks the adults use to sneak around.

"Too far," Lisa whispers as the dark water beside them stirs. There's a strong current running in the opposite direction, but there's something down there, following them in the river, fighting to keep pace as they move upstream.

Jenny sees it too. Her shoe slips on some loose rocks and several stones cascade down into the water, causing a flurry of excitement. Too much excitement for her.

"I'm going back," she says.

"It's there. It's right there," Deon says, pointing. *There* is another hundred yards away, following the curve of the river. They could cut across the U-shaped bend to shorten the distance, but that would mean risking themselves in the open.

"What's down *there?*" Lisa asks, pointing at the river. Like Jenny, she's more interested in what's here than what's over there, and not out of idle curiosity. Both girls are scared.

Deon looks. He doesn't know, that much is obvious from his carefree demeanor.

"Monsters," Jenny says.

"There are no monsters. Come on. In five minutes, you'll be eating candy and wondering what all the fuss was about."

Jenny and Lisa look at each other. Deon's already following the track along the riverbank, weaving in and out of the thick bushes.

"He could be walking into a trap," Lisa says. She's right. Jenny looks back at the crumbled buildings providing them with sanctuary and realizes Deon's also right. There's no certainty in life. No guarantees anywhere. They hide in holes in the ground, fooling themselves into thinking they're safe. With the lights out, they pretend they're safe, but they're not.

"You know what's funny?" she says to Lisa. "Back there, down in the basement, the noises from the war scare me. They're the same out here. Louder even, but they don't scare me."

"Why not?"

"I don't know. Maybe because I can see stuff. I can see the battle's over there. Down below, it feels as though there are monsters creeping up on me."

Lisa nods. She must feel the same way.

"Come on," Jenny says, starting down the track after Deon.

"What if there is something out there? A monster?"

Jenny smiles, saying, "It'll get him first," and she's only half kidding. If there are monsters, Deon's her coal mine canary.

Weeds grow out of the path. Rats scurry away through the undergrowth. Their aquatic friend follows for a while, but seems to lose interest, or at least it wants them to think it's lost interest. Regardless, Jenny sticks to the inside of the path, closest to the bank, not wanting to risk sliding into the water in the dark.

They watch as Deon crawls behind a concrete slab. A building on the far side of the park has collapsed into the river. The upper floors have fallen like gigantic dominos. The slabs are cracked and uneven, but largely intact, lying on each other.

"In here."

Jenny follows, wondering how Deon knew about this place, and wondering why they couldn't have snuck away in the daylight to explore the building.

Moonlight drifts in through the shattered upper floor. The roof has collapsed, but he's right. Inside, there's a 7-11 sign on the floor, along with crushed shelving. Most of the packaging either split open during the collapse or has been nibbled at by mice. There's a soda machine and a Slurpee dispenser.

"Oh, man," Deon says. "Can you imagine if this still worked?"

"That would be cool," Lisa says, smiling at the thought.

Jenny catches some movement in the shadows beside her, and her heart skips a beat. She turns, seeing a dark figure against the wall, and laughs.

"It's a mirror," she says, looking at her dim reflection.

Lisa chimes up with, "Mirror, mirror on the wall. Who's the fairest of them all?"

"Will you be serious?" Deon asks.

"There's a storeroom," Jenny says, pushing on a steel door. It creaks as it opens, which sends a shiver down her spine.

Deon pulls out his flashlight. Like most of the kids, he has a windup light. Forty to fifty cranks and the tiny LED light will be good for half an hour. It's not something they can use outside for fear of being spotted, but in here it's ideal for exploring. The soft light ripples across buckled shelves and crushed cardboard boxes, and—

"No," Deon says. "No, no, no..."

The soft-white glow reveals a monster.

~*~

Machines & Monsters

TENTACLES REACH FOR the light. A single compound eye stares at them, swaying on a stalk protruding from a gelatinous blob. The body of the creature is flattened, as if Earth's gravity is too much for it to bear.

All three teens briefly freeze. Slowly, they back away, easing out of the storeroom, not taking their eyes off the monster. Tentacles flex and wave, stretching out toward a machine that's toppled against the fallen shelves.

Once they're back in the 7-11, they run, scrambling out from behind the concrete slab and into the night. The teens sprint, pumping their legs and madly swinging their arms as they race along the riverbank. Within a hundred yards, they're wheezing, gasping for breath. They stop beneath the shattered remains of the overpass, taking shelter in the shadows.

Jenny leans forward on her knees, sucking in air. Lisa paces back and forth, mumbling. Deon's laughing.

"Did you see that?" he asks. "Did you see that thing?"

Lisa says, "The monster? Ah. Yeah. I saw it."

"That really was a monster," Deon says, shaking his head. "We found one. For real. A real live monster. Damn."

"How did it get in there?" Jenny asks.

Deon points back at the fallen building. "Must have been in there when the floors came down."

Between breaths, Jenny asks, "How long has it been—trapped?"

"I dunno," Deon says. "Days. Weeks. Months. I'm not sure."

"What are we going to do?"

"We've got to tell our folks," Lisa says.

"They'll kill it," Jenny replies.

"Well, yeah," Deon says. "That's the general idea when it comes to war. You kill your enemies."

Jenny is unusually calm. "Did you see the way it looked at us? It was scared."

"Scared? *I* was scared," Lisa says. "I was trying not to piss my pants."

Deon laughs.

"I'm serious," Jenny says. "I don't think it meant us any harm."

"How do you know that?" Deon asks. "Do you speak monster alien?"

Lisa says, "It could be poisonous."

"Then we won't eat it."

"You know what I mean. It could be dangerous."

Jenny is resolute. "No more dangerous than creeping around a riverbank in the middle of a war."

"You want to go back there?" Deon asks, picking up on her reasoning.

"Why not?"

"It could kill us," Lisa protests.

"It couldn't kill us. Did you see that thing? It doesn't have any bones. It's an introvert."

"Invertebrate," Deon says, correcting Jenny.

"Whatever."

"What if it slits your throat?" Lisa asks.

"What if it doesn't?" Jenny replies, surprising herself. Coming face to face with a monster has dispelled her fears. That pathetic creature trapped in the storeroom is the antithesis of all her expectations. There were no fangs, no claws, no snarling or growling. "We could learn something. Think about it. No one's ever seen one of these things before... What do you do when you see a pretty beetle on a rock pile? Do you step on it and squish it? Or do you take pity on it and put it on the grass?"

"I'm not touching it," Lisa says.

"That's not what I meant."

"I'll go back," Deon says.

Lisa is defiant. "I'm not going anywhere near that monster."

"Come on then," Jenny says, turning to Deon.

"Wait," Lisa calls out, trying not to be too loud, but Jenny and Deon are already bending beneath shrubs and working their way back to the fallen building. "Guys?" Down below, the water stirs, and Lisa's decision is made for her. "I'm coming too."

Quietly, the three teens creep back into the shadow of the fallen building, stepping carefully on the floor, dodging plastic wrappers and empty cans scattered across the linoleum.

Jenny whispers, "Have you got your flashlight?" Deon hands it to her and she winds the crank. There's movement in response to the sound. The creature is restless, thrashing around in the dark.

"Easy," Jenny says, inching forward with the flashlight illuminating the door to the storeroom. "We're not going to hurt you."

"Not yet," Lisa whispers, positioning herself behind Deon. She picks up a hunk of wood, holding it like a baseball bat.

For his part, Deon has his hands on Jenny's waist, creeping along behind her. He whispers, "This is stupid, really stupid. Even for me."

"Shhhh," Jenny says, peering inside the storeroom and shining the light on the monster. The creature reacts, hissing and extending its tentacles like spears reaching out in all directions.

"There, are you happy?" Lisa whispers.

"It's afraid," Jenny says.

"I'm afraid. It's a monster. Monsters know no fear."

"And yet it does," Deon says. They watch as the creature flexes back and forth, but it never moves more than a few inches. "It's trapped."

"Look at the shelves." Jenny runs the light around the room. The monster's body is pinned by the fallen shelves. The weight of its own machine, bearing down on the shelves, has ensnared it. "Give me a hand."

"You're not serious?" Lisa asks, watching tentacles wave through the air. Jenny hands Lisa the flashlight while she and Deon pull at the machine, which resembles a fridge without handles. Lisa panics, shaking as she holds the flashlight on the creature. "It's going to eat us."

"It's *not* going to eat us," Deon replies. "Look at the size of it. Damn thing is smaller than a cat."

The alien remains still, with its one eye intently watching the children, apparently understanding what they're trying to do. They can't lift the machine, but they can push it to one side so it crashes down on the floor beside them.

With the weight off the shelving, the creature can move. It climbs by slapping tentacles against the drywall and hauling itself up. Within seconds, it's hanging from the ceiling, with its tentacles splayed wide and its body sagging. One strange eye hangs upside down, watching them with curiosity. Unlike an octopus, the creature has dozens of arms instead of six to eight.

"Can we go now?" Lisa asks, her voice trembling. "I need to pee. I really need to go. Now."

"It looks like a squid," Deon says.

Jenny takes the flashlight from Lisa, holding it steady on the creature. The alien sways, not liking the light. Each of its tentacles moves independently. They ripple, flexing as the monster moves across the ceiling.

"It's going for the machine," Jenny says, backing up. As they watch, the alien drops, plopping onto the smooth white surface of the machine. There are cracks around the edges of the panels, barely a quarter of an inch wide but running the length of the box. To their amazement, the alien squeezes through the tiny gap, twisting and contorting its body and squishing its tentacles, its torso, and finally its eye through the impossibly thin space.

"Woah," Deon says.

"Can we leave, please?" Lisa asks, tugging on Jenny's shirt.

"Look at that!" Deon points at thousands of spindly arms protruding through the gaps in the machine. These aren't tentacles, though. They're mechanical, not biological. The thin spikes move independently, covering all the edges of the box. Suddenly, it's no longer a fallen refrigerator—it's alive. The box scurries across the floor with a surprising amount of speed, and Lisa jumps, screaming. The machine uses the wall to climb, righting itself. Hundreds of tiny pinpricks mark where spikes dig into the wall. With the box upright, the spikes retract from everywhere except the base.

Lisa whimpers. Her dress is wet. A puddle forms on the floor by her feet.

"I'm scared," she says. "I'm really scared."

"Me too," Deon says.

"I'm not." Jenny has found courage in curiosity. When monsters lurked in the dark, they were scary. When they seemed to creep up on her in the depths of the basement parking lot, they were terrifying. In her imagination, they had claws and teeth, and threatened to devour her, but facing an actual alien has quelled her fears. She sees the creature as alive, mortal, not supernatural—it's hurt and afraid, she's not.

"Yeah, time to go," Deon says, backing into the store as the white monolith glides to the door on a sea of tiny legs.

"Don't you want to see what it's going to do?" Jenny asks.

Lisa says, "I want to see the sun rise."

The three teens retreat to the edge of the fallen slab. The machine moves around the store, ignoring them. Although all four sides look the same, the box appears to have a sense of direction. It goes over to the Slurpee machine. Thin spikes and tentacles probe at the broken drink dispenser.

"Look," Jenny says. Colored lights appear behind the cracked plastic on the Slurpee machine. A large screw turns even though there's no fluid in the container. Tentacles reach from the safety of the white box, turning a tap on the wall. Water flows into the dispenser, but it's dirty.

Lisa says, "It's fixing it."

"Why?" Deon asks. The white machine busies itself, moving through the 7-11, examining the cash register and a busted TV screen. It's trying to fix anything that's broken. Dozens of thin spikes manipulate an old computer case with astonishing dexterity. Screws are pulled from the back panel. The circuit board is exposed, along with electrical wiring and the power supply.

Lisa says, "I don't like it."

"Why isn't it leaving?" Deon asks. "We're at war, right? Shouldn't it be trying to get back to its own people?"

"People?" Jenny asks, remembering stories about the people the aliens deprived of free will.

Deon creeps forward, wanting to get a better look at the machine. "It's ignoring us."

Lisa says, "We should leave—before it slits our throats."

"Doesn't it seem strange to you?" Jenny asks.

"It *is* strange to me," Lisa says, interrupting her.

"No, I mean, think about it. We're at war. We have artillery and guns, armored personnel carriers and bombs."

"They have refrigerators," Deon says, completing her thought.

"Exactly."

"Where are their tanks?" Lisa asks.

"Good question," Deon says, and Jenny senses some of Lisa's fear fading. She's growing curious.

The machine begins straightening boxes, picking up scraps of paper and piling them on the bench. It's hypnotic to watch candy wrappers being passed between hundreds of tiny legs as they're lifted from the floor and placed on the counter. To Jenny's mind, it's like watching a centipede clean up.

"This thing couldn't cut anyone's throat," she says. Neither Deon nor Lisa reply. "It couldn't even fit down the aisle between our bunks."

There's a voice outside—a radio. A flashlight flickers over the concrete, exposing the gap in the slab. Jenny turns off her light. The kids hide in the storeroom, peering out from the darkness as a soldier climbs over the rubble and slips through the cracked concrete into the store.

"There you are," she says. The machine turns. Hundreds of tiny legs scurry across the linoleum floor. The soldier holds out her hand, pressing lightly against the white panels as dozens of spikes reach for her. "I got your signal. Where have you been? Are you okay?"

Thin tentacles reach from beneath one of the panels. The soldier removes her gloves. A tentacle wraps around her hand, winding their way around the woman's forearm. "It's okay. I know. You were scared. You were trapped. But I'm here now. Let's get you out of this place."

In the pitch black of the storeroom, Lisa steps on some shelving lying on the floor. It's metal, and it clatters around. In an instant, the soldier has her rifle leveled at the storeroom.

"Who's there?"

She cocks the gun, pulling back on the bolt and loading a round into the chamber of a plasma blaster.

"Show yourself," she says, "or I will incinerate that room," but the machine trundles in front of her, blocking her view. "What are you doing?" she asks the machine, trying to line up a clear shot around the side of the alien refrigerator. The machine shifts sideways, keeping itself between her and the teens.

Jenny creeps out of the darkness and peers past the alien machine. She has her hands raised. Deon follows her, with his arms raised high. He could catch the ceiling should it fall. Lastly, Lisa sulks forward.

"Kids?" the soldier says, slipping her rifle back on her shoulder. "You're just children. What are you doing out here after dark?"

Jenny hangs her head.

Deon says, "We were—looking for candy."

"Candy?" the soldier asks, laughing. "Well, you didn't find *candy*, did you?" She gestures to the machine. "Did you find him in there?"

Jenny nods, still not making eye contact.

"You freed him?"

She nods again, feeling as though she's done something wrong.

"Are you going to kill us?" Deon asks.

"I'm not going to hurt you," the soldier says, crouching and beckoning for the kids to come forward into the moonlight. The alien machine moves to one side, apparently finding something interesting over by the crushed remains of the stairwell.

"She's going to cut our throats," Lisa whispers.

"No one's going to—" but the soldier stops mid-sentence. "What do you know about them?"

"The monsters?" Jenny asks, pointing at the machine as it dismantles a soda dispenser, methodically removing parts and piling them neatly on the ground.

The soldier hoists herself up on the bench, sitting with her legs crossed. She places her rifle beside her and reaches into her pocket, pulling out a granola bar. "Monsters are evil. That's obvious, right? Big and scary. Nasty. But this guy's not really a monster, is he?"

The teens nod in agreement. She tosses them the granola bar. Deon catches it.

"It's not a trick," she says. "We're not monsters."

Deon tears open the package and takes a bite, offering some to Jenny. She tears off a chunk and hands the rest to Lisa, who looks at the bar carefully before shaking her head and handing it back to Deon.

"The worst of all monsters are the ones that smile. You look at this creature and see something unnatural, by our standards. You see a monster. I see an ally. A friend. The real monsters are those that would cut your throats in your sleep."

"Why would anyone do that to children?" Jenny asks.

"Why indeed," the soldier replies.

Deon says, "Because they're afraid."

The soldier nods her head, asking, "Of what?"

"Of losing control."

The soldier points at him. "Yes."

Jenny's mind casts back to the basement and the conversation between the adults. "Mom?" She wipes away a tear. "My mom?"

"I'm sorry, kiddo. I know you didn't ask to be born on the wrong side of history, but shit happens."

"But—but that can't be true. It just can't."

Lisa says, "My mom would never do that."

"You have to understand," the soldier says. "The toughest thing for anyone to admit is that they might be wrong. Your mom is doing what she thinks is right. They all are. That's the crazy thing. This is us. This is our history. Always thinking we're right. Back in 1776, the British thought they were right. The Civil War. World War One. World War Two. Korea. Vietnam. Iraq. Afghanistan. No one's ever fought for a side they thought was wrong."

Jenny doesn't know where most of these countries are, or even if they still exist.

"But they took our free will," she says.

"Is that what they told you?" The soldier shakes her head. "You've seen it right? The squid. You've seen it outside its machine. Is it really that scary?"

The teens shake their heads.

"Look at what it's doing. Does it look like it's trying to take over the world?"

"No," Deon says.

"It's trying to fix things," Lisa says.

"Exactly. Only some of us don't want things fixed."

Jenny stutters, "But—but we're wrong? We can't be wrong."

"Do you want to know a secret?" the soldier asks. "Do you want to know what the scariest thing in the world really is?"

Jenny and Deon look at each other, unsure if they really want to know.

"It's not monsters or alien machines… It's change."

"What are you going to do with us?" Jenny asks.

"Me?" the soldier asks in reply, pointing at herself and then the machine. "I came here for him, not you." She chews on another granola bar. "Trippy, huh? The big bad guys that want to take away your freedom not taking away your freedom."

"So, we can go?" Deon asks.

The soldier points at the crack in the concrete, saying, "Be careful out there. Keep your heads down. Stay in the shadows." The three kids look at each other. "Watch out for monsters. Real monsters."

Suddenly, no one wants to leave.

"It doesn't have to be this way," the soldier says. "I was once—"

A flash of intense, white light cuts through the air, ripping from the back of the store to the front in a fraction of the time it takes Jenny's heart to beat just once. She feels a wave of heat radiate from the pulse. She cringes, ducking even though the bolt has already passed. The soldier keels backwards, tumbling behind the counter as the plasma round strikes her like a lightning bolt. Ash drifts from the shelves behind her. The smell of burning flesh fills the air.

"Quick, children."

"Mom?" Jenny calls out. She's in shock at the sudden burst of violence, the abrupt change from life to death. She trembles.

Her mother steps forward into the moonlight. Steam rises from the barrel of her rifle, wafting into the cool air. How long has she been standing there in the shadows? How much did she hear?

"We need to move out before reinforcements arrive."

"Mom!" Jenny yells, more in horror than relief. Her mother holds her hand out for her daughter, beckoning her closer.

"Come with me. Now."

Susan Culpepper hasn't seen the machine. In the midst of the chaos in the store, it looks like part of the shelving, almost as though it were a display case. Then she catches its motion, seeing hundreds of legs sweeping along as the creature scurries toward the fallen soldier. Susan Culpepper swings her gun around and fires another plasma round. Jenny moves in unison with her, realizing what's happening, and steps in front of the incoming fire bolt, yelling, "No!"

The blast hits Jenny in the center of her chest, burning a hole clear through her ribcage, searing her internal organs, and reducing her heart and lungs to a seething mess of bloody pulp. Smoke billows into the air.

Jenny falls to her knees. She looks at her smoldering clothes and scorched flesh. The crater in her chest defies belief, but there it is, still bubbling and boiling under the intensity of the heat. She chokes, unable to breathe, and collapses face first on the linoleum. Strangely, there's no pain. A mixture of shock and severe nerve damage spares her the agony of those last, fleeting seconds.

"Jenny!" her mother yells, dropping the rifle and running to her side. Susan rolls Jenny over. Already, her daughter's eyes have a glazed look. Jenny's neck and jaw go slack, and she slumps in her mother's arms. Dead.

Susan Culpepper flinches as a rifle barrel digs into the back of her shoulder. She turns, seeing the soldier towering over her.

"Get away from the girl," the soldier says, barely able to stand. Blood drips from a burn on her shoulder. Her left arm hangs limp by her side. The muscle has been torn away. Scorch marks reach to the white of her bones.

"She's my daughter," Susan protests. The soldier kicks Susan, prodding her with the rifle, and she relents. Deon and Lisa slump against the wall, sliding down so they're sitting on the linoleum with their backs to the storeroom.

The machine advances on Jenny's body.

"Don't you touch her, you monster," Susan yells.

The soldier plants her boot on Susan's shoulder, shoving her against the wall next to the kids. She has the barrel of her rifle inches from her head. "You're the monster."

Hundreds of spindly arms protrude from the gaps lining the alien machine, grabbing at Jenny's body and hauling it up so her frame is held against the white outer panel. Tentacles writhe from within, coming from the top of the box almost seven feet in height. To Susan Culpepper's horror, they begin feeling their way down toward her daughter's lifeless body. She holds her hand over her mouth as the bulbous alien with its solitary eye on a thin stalk creeps out of the machine.

The soldier keeps both her rifle and her eyes on Susan, turning her back to the creature.

"No, please," Susan says.

"Mrs. Culpepper," Deon says. "You don't understand." But it's not that Susan doesn't understand, it's that she doesn't *want* to understand. For Susan Culpepper, there's right and wrong. There's good and bad. There are angels and devils. She knows what's right, and no one can tell her otherwise.

The alien smothers the young girl, clambering over her face. Tentacles wrap around her neck, slithering over her shoulders. Jenny is being held aloft by hundreds of tiny spikes coming out of either side of the box, holding her with spider-like arms. Blood seeps from pinpricks on her shoulders, marking where the spikes are digging into her skin.

The slimy creature positions itself over the smoldering cavity in the middle of Jenny's chest. The alien nestles into the wound. It pulsates, pumping with the rhythm of a heart. Tentacles spread out across Jenny's shoulders and neck, reaching down beneath her burnt clothing to her waist. Several tentacles disappear inside her nose and mouth.

"Leave her. Let her be," Susan shouts. The soldier pushes the barrel of her gun into Susan's shoulder, suggesting she's more than willing to return the favor if Susan tries to intervene.

Seconds pass like days. Susan sobs, burying her head in her hands. The soldier steps back, resting the rifle on the counter as she applies a field dressing to her exposed shoulder muscle.

It takes almost five minutes, but Jenny's eyes open wide in shock, staring straight ahead. She gasps, choking. Tentacles withdraw from her mouth and she breathes. She looks down at the alien embedded in her chest and panics, pulling herself away from the machine. The spikes release her, and she staggers forward with the alien functioning as her heart and lungs.

"I—I," she says, with her hands poised over the creature covering the wound in her chest. A single alien eye stares up at her. Sticky, gooey mucus seeps from around the edge of her exposed ribcage. The alien flattens itself, pulsating and slowly filling the wound entirely. The tentacles lining her face wrap themselves around her neck. Jenny touches at them gently and they respond, curling around her fingers.

"You're a—a monster," her mother says.

"I'm a—I'm alive," she replies, barely able to speak.

Jenny staggers, unsure of her own legs. Her feet are clumsy. Deon and Lisa rush over, grabbing her.

"Hey, it's okay." Deon was always overly optimistic.

Lisa screws up her face at the prospect of being so close to the alien, but she loves her friend. And yet she can't take her eyes of the alien pumping blood around Jenny's body.

"You should see yourself. You look—"

"Awful?"

"Amazing."

If she could, Jenny would laugh. She sees the extent of her injuries in the mirror. The alien has buried itself in an area roughly a foot in diameter, consuming most of her chest from her shoulders to her stomach. The pulsating mass providing her with life is strangely comforting rather than distressing.

Deon asks, "What do you see?"

Jenny's eyes settle on the reflection of the dull blue, cold, slimy alien skin as she says, "The fairest of them all."

Lisa squeezes Jenny's waist.

"On your feet," the soldier says, kicking Susan.

"What are you going to do with us?"

"What happens next is up to you." She kicks Susan's gun into the storeroom, and waves the barrel of her rifle toward the gap in the concrete slab. "Move."

Deon and Lisa help Jenny, clambering over the rubble and out into the night. Susan follows, with the soldier hanging back behind her. They step out into moonlight and the path divides, with one section leading back to the plaza and the other carrying on toward the hills.

"Which way are you going?" the soldier asks. "Two years ago, I was where you are now. I was hiding in holes in the ground, fighting a war I believed in, but belief is not enough. I was wrong."

Susan remains silent.

"Do you know what the aliens changed?"

Susan doesn't reply. Her eyes are fixed on the creature embedded in her daughter's chest.

"Nothing. They didn't change a goddamn thing. Sometimes, I wish they had. We changed. We finally saw the tribes we cling to for what they are—pathetic relics of our primitive past. You're fighting for freedom from tyrants that don't exist. You're fighting your own paranoia. We're fighting for change."

She slips her rifle over her shoulder and starts walking away, down the track toward the dark mountains. Deon and Lisa follow, half-carrying Jenny between them.

"Wait," Susan Culpepper calls out. "You're just going to leave me here?"

No one replies.

"Jenny?"

Susan Culpepper has a decision to make. What's more important, her pride or her daughter? She looks back at the shattered buildings dominating the skyline, noticing for the first time how they resemble a cemetery. Those crumbling, broken tombstones speak only of the dead. She turns and follows her daughter into the night.

The End

~*~

Afterword

Thank you for your kind support of independent science fiction. *Mirror, Mirror* is a tribute to an episode of *The Twilight Zone* called *The Monsters are Due on Maple Street*.

I love the way *The Monsters are Due on Maple Street* used the concept of role-reversal, and I wanted to emulate the same idea in this story. We're used to seeing stories from the vantage point of the good guys, so it's interesting to explore life from the perspective of someone caught on the wrong side of history, and consider the challenges they face when they honestly confront their motives.

I think the best stories are a story within a story. How did Susan and Jenny end up in that basement carpark in the first place? I don't know. What will happen to Jenny now she's on extraterrestrial life-support? Again, I don't know, but that's what makes the story resonate for me. It's a small glimpse into a fictional world, a chance to enjoy seeing life from another angle.

If you've enjoyed this short story, be sure to check out my novels online, or look me up on Twitter and Facebook.

Cheers,
Peter Cawdron

~*~

The Lost Tapes–
The Madness of
King Street

Daniel Arthur Smith

~*~

"*RECORDING BEGINS with today's date, October 6th 2017. My name is Agent Melissa Muldoon. Present with me is Agent Lawrence Meyer. Commencing interview of sole surviving witness of the September 4th incident at King Street Station, one Mister Sean Bellar. Mister Bellar, can you please state your name for the record?*"

"Sure. Right in here?"

"*No need to lean forward. Just speak clearly.*"

"Sorry."

"*It's all right. Your name please.*"

"Sean Bellar."

"*Thank you, Mister Bellar. Up front, I have to tell you that we were a bit excited to meet with you today. I'm a big fan of your work. I've seen The Bartender at least a half dozen times.*"

"Oh. I'm glad you enjoyed it."

"Yeah. I admit I like the romances. Agent Meyer here likes the action movies, though. His favorite is Soldier of Fortune. Isn't that right, Larry?"

"Those are fun, too."

"Tsk. I just wish we were meeting under better circumstances. Thank you for being so...onboard...with the investigation."

"Of course. I mean...I don't know how I can help, really. I already told Agent Meyer everything."

"And we appreciate that, but for the record, we need to hear–in your own words–what happened at the King Street station."

"I don't know what else I could tell you. Did you see them...the bodies I mean?"

"We're conducting a full forensic investigation. We need this recording for the official report."

"Oh...I don't suppose I could have a drink?"

"Of course. Larry can you get Mister Bellar some water—"

"I was thinking something a little stiffer."

"Sorry. We can't..."

"No. I guess not."

"We can give you some aspirin. Those bandages on your shoulder and side, I bet you're sore."

"That would be great."

"Thanks, Larry. This will help. Drink it up. Take a breath. Okay?"

"Yeah."

"Excellent. So, let's continue the interview. Can you please tell us what happened?"

"Where do I start?"

"How about start with telling us what you were doing at the King Street station?"

"I was looking for a friend."

"Would that be Eldon Conroy?"

"Yes. I was looking for Eldon."

"A bit more than friends. Wouldn't you say?"

"How do you—"

"Your business is our business."

"Of course."

"Don't worry. Your secrets are safe with us. We just want to hear what happened."

"Right."

"So, you were looking for your friend, Eldon Conroy."

"Yes. We'd gotten into an argument."

"About what?"

"Uh…About him being a secret I guess."

"I see. And you figured he went to the King Street station?"

"No, no. I'm sorry. We were flying home when the argument happened."

"From what location?"

"From the islands. He sometimes joins me when I'm shooting, it breaks up the monotony. You'd be surprised how boring a film set can be. Anyway, the last I saw him was at customs."

"You were separated?"

"No, I…Because of being who I am, I was able to express through. He usually stays by my side. But he was angry, and went into a separate line. He's incredibly passive aggressive. He did it just so I'd have to wait. But I didn't. Wait, I mean. I left him behind. I expected he'd be a half hour behind me. He never came home."

"Why did you think he'd be at the station?"

"When he didn't come home, I called some friends. No one had seen him. So, I used the search app, on the phone."

"Search app?"

"The one that tells you where a cell phone is. 'Find your Phone' or whatever."

"You were able to search for 'his' phone? How is that possible?"

"I pay for his phone. It's under my account."

"That's how you keep tabs on him?"

"No. It's not like that. I know it sounds like that. Like I was stalking him. I wasn't. I felt bad. I'd been mean. I wanted to apologize. Anyway, he must've taken the train from the airport because the app put his location at King Street station, just two blocks from home. So, I decided I'd meet up with him."

"Did you?"

"Did I what?"

"Meet up with him?"

"I don't know."

"What do you mean you don't know?"

"I told Agent Meyer. Things were hazy. You know, I'm just a regular guy. I mean, I play the hero, but I'm an actor."

"Things were hazy at the terminal?"

"Yes. I mean, I was fine when I arrived."

"What time was that?"

"Dusk. Nine maybe."

"When did you stop being fine? Explain in detail please. This will be incredibly helpful."

"The streets were clear. Not too many people downtown. There never are after rush hour. I remember it was dusk because I was thinking—as I approached the station—that it was magnificent the way the twilight hued from a fuchsia to a deep blue behind the winged spires."

"It is an amazing building."

"Amazing all right. It looks like a giant bird of bone and glass. The way those back-lit white ribs spike up into the sky like huge wings. Absolutely visionary."

"So, you remember admiring the architecture? What else?"

"Yeah. I clearly remember thinking how amazing the new station is, and I remember entering and thinking that there were a lot of people in there—as opposed to the empty street."

"What were they doing?"

"The people?"

"Yes. I take it that nothing appeared out of the ordinary?"

"No. Nothing at all. The promenade up top was empty. Just the bone white ribs towering up like a cathedral. But people peppered the floor of the mall below. There were people at the macaroon stand and at the flower stand—the Bouquet Bar—and there were janitors mopping. People funneled through from the platforms and into the cafes and shops to the sides."

"And that was clear?"

"Clear?"

"Not yet hazy?"

"Yeah. It was clear. Fine. It was when I as I was riding down the escalator that things…"

"Things what?"

"Do you think we were drugged? Was it terrorists?"

"That's what you're going to help us find out. What happened on the escalator?"

"Nothing really. Half way down, I saw Eldon. He was at a little bar to the right. I thought I'd find him there. They stock a rosé from the Côtes de Provence that he can't resist. And sure enough, there he was, at a café table, still wearing his light blue linen blazer—his red carry-on at his feet. I was looking at him when he saw me. He smiled, and then…"

"And then?"

"I felt a tingling, like when the sun hits your skin, and I looked up to the strip of glass that runs the length of the station between where the wings come together."

"What did you see?"

"Moonlight. I saw the light of the moon. That's when things became…"

"Hazy?"

"Yeah."

"Do you have any memories at all of what happened next?"

"In a blur. There was tingling, a wave of nausea, and then it was as if my flesh was ripping away. I fell, and I couldn't move and someone was screaming, this loud unnatural wail that made my head split. It wouldn't stop and I looked around to see where it was coming from, one of—no both—of the janitors ran toward me. One crouched beside me. An Asian man. He reached out to help me and that's when I realized where the screaming was coming from."

"And where was it coming from?"

"The screaming was coming from me. And then…"

"Then?"

"The janitor, his face crumpled, distorted, panicked. He jolted, dropped onto his ass, and back pedaled away from me. He was—he was scared of something. He scurried back, and the screaming stopped. And then—but that can't be right. How did I not remember that before? Ha. I had this crazy dream."

"You were in shock. Go ahead, have another drink. The water is helping…There you go."

"Where was I?"

"The screaming stopped."

"Right. The screaming stopped. Sudden like. I must have passed out. That's where it's hazy again. Like a dream, but lucid. The janitor was crawling away from me as fast as he could, but backwards, like a crab. And, in my dream—and this is the crazy part—I somehow flew across the mall from the bottom of the escalator where I fell and landed right on top of him—and bit him on the neck. Except in the dream, my jaws sliced right through—flesh, bone, and all—and decapitated him. I know it sounds nuts, but I must've have seen something and my brain put it together in a weird string."

"A weird string?"

"Yeah. A weird string of events. I suppose I've seen so many special effects sets that my mind got away with me. I mean, I dreamed I took out the other janitor after the first, I impaled him with a long stick—a spear I guess."

"He was impaled with the handle of his mop."

"Excuse me?"

"The on-scene investigators wrote that Jose Garmo was impaled with the handle of his broom."

"So, it wasn't a dream. I must've witnessed the whole thing."

"What else did you witness?"

"Ah…Dirt flying, jars of flowers hurling from the Bouquet Bar. The girl behind the counter, mutilated, her arm wrenched from her body, torn away as easily as a stuffed teddy bear."

"I'm sure it was dreadful."

"Yes. Yes, it was dreadful. I don't really remember clearly, you understand. I must've been heavily drugged. But I do remember seeing all of those people, torn limb from limb, and then I must've fully blacked out. Because I don't remember anything else with clarity—a glimpse of the ambulance, lights above me when they wheeled me in. That's it until I woke up here."

"Nothing else?"

"No. I told you, it was crazy. I wasn't even aware that anyone was hurt until Agent Meyer told me."

"Did he tell you?"

"Well he said he wanted to know what happened. To the people, I mean."

"Hmmm. That's what you remember?"

"Well. Maybe not exactly. Hey. Are we done here? I mean, I can tell you again if you like, if that's what you need. Whatever it takes to catch these guys. But I really don't know anything else. You must have video. Can't you just see what happened?"

"We do."

"Than can you tell me what happened?"

"On the evening of October 5th an alarm was triggered at King Street station. Three minutes later, police arrived and entered the terminal. There, they discovered a large animal. The creature charged the police, was shot, and then collapsed. At 10:15 p.m., the police radioed all clear. On-scene investigators reported dead bodies everywhere."

"That's horrible. Where's Eldon? Is he okay? Is he here waiting for me?"

"I'm sorry, Mister Bellar. According to the video you asked about, everyone in the station was killed, by the creature. Everyone except you."

"No. That can't be right. This is madness"

"Mister Bellar, were you injured in any way when you were filming?"

"Yeah."

"Was it a bite of some kind?"

"A drunk. We were filming a night scene and some drunk snuck onto the set. How did you know?"

"Call it a guess, Mister Bellar. Agent Meyer is going to take you back to your...room. Larry, can you please help Mister Bellar out."

~*~

"Hello, Director Higgins. You saw the interview?"

"Sean Bellar. I wouldn't have missed it."

"You think he's lying or in denial?"

"Oh, he's in denial. Very rarely are those affected by the virus even aware of what happens during a full moon."

"It's a shame. He doesn't even remember being shot."

"What about the drunk he mentioned?"

"The 'drunk' on the set was a lover in his trailer. That's what his partner was upset about. We apprehended him this morning. He tested positive, as did his partner and the other two survivors."

"There can't be any survivors."

"Understood. What about Mister Bellar?"

"Him too, unfortunately. Records will show he died during the incident. Lose the recording."

"Yes, sir."

"You know, I enjoyed *The Bartender* too—that was a great film."

~*~

ABOUT THE AUTHORS

Christopher J. Valin is a writer, teacher, artist, and historian living in the Los Angeles area. He received his masters' degree with honors in military history from American Military University and his bachelor's degree in history from the University of Colorado-Colorado Springs. Christopher is the 5x-great-grandson of Sir Charles Douglas, the subject of his book, Fortune's Favorite: Sir Charles and the Breaking of the Line.

In addition to writing and inking for independent comic book companies and writing screenplays for production companies, Christopher has had numerous short stories published in anthologies such as *Clockwork & Capes: Superheroes in the Age of Steam* and *Doomed: Tales of the Last Days*. His screenplays, teleplays, and stories have won several awards and contests.

For more information, visit christophervalin.com

Kevin Lauderdale has written essays and articles for the *Los Angeles Times*, *The Dictionary of American Biography*, and **McSweeneys.net**. His short fiction has appeared in several of Pocket Books' *Star Trek* anthologies as well as various small press publications. His story "Box 27" was published in the science journal *Nature*. This is his fourth appearance in Canyons of the Damned. He hosts the Old Time Radio podcast, *"Presenting the Transcription Feature,"* and co-hosts *"Temple of Bad,"* the podcast about movies that are so bad, they're practically a religious experience, both on the Chronic Rift network. He is a member of SFWA and HWA.

For more information, visit
kevinlauderale.livejournal.com

Lara Frater, published a non-fiction book *Fat Chicks Rule! How to Survive a Thin Centric World*. It was a guidebook on being a big girl in a thin world and included information on how to fat positive books, movies, and TV, where to find fashion, comfortable seating, and how to deal with fat hatred. A few months after the book was published, I did a companion blog with the same name that she still updates every Monday.

She has published essays, poetry and short stories.

In 2012, she published *End of the Line* the first in the series of three zombie novels that take place in a world almost dead of the flu and having to deal the zombies who rose from the ashes. *End of the Line* was followed by *Stuck in the Middle* in 2013 and *Full Circle* in 2014.

She is also working on a three book dystopian series called *Welcome to Pluto*. I hope to have the first book out in 2016.

She lives in New York City with her husband, author Jonathan Frater and has lots of animals and people in her house.

Peter Cawdron is an Australian science fiction writer, specializing in hard science fiction. Hard science fiction is a misnomer as far as categories of literature go, as it sounds harsh and difficult to understand, but that is far from reality. Hard science fiction is simply plausible science fiction, fiction that is written in such a way as it conforms to the known laws of science, and that makes it more interesting, as there's no magic wand the protagonist can wave to get out of trouble. Peter's forays into hard science fiction could best be described as informative science fiction or enjoyable science fiction. Peter is a fan of such classic science fiction writers as Philip K. Dick, Arthur C. Clarke and Michael Crichton and their influence on his style and story lines is readily apparent.

For more information, visit thinkingscifi.wordpress.com

Daniel Arthur Smith is a USA Today bestselling author. His titles include *Spectral Shift, Hugh Howey Lives, The Cathari Treasure, The Somali Deception*, and a few other novels and short stories. He also curates the phenomenal short fiction series *Tales from the Canyons of the Damned*.

He was raised in Michigan and graduated from Western Michigan University where he studied philosophy, with focus on cognitive science, meta-physics, and comparative religion. He began his career as a bartender, barista, poetry house proprietor, teacher, and then became a technologist and futurist for the Fortune 100 across the Americas and Europe.

Daniel has traveled to over 300 cities in 22 countries, residing in Los Angeles, Kalamazoo, Prague, Crete, and now writes in Manhattan where he lives with his wife and young sons.

For more information, visit danielarthursmith.com

~*~